Despite the recent loss of his parents, Ash Woodhart is content living with his siblings, deep in the southern countryside of his family's domain. Ren, an aloof boy with no home and no family, is an intrusion forced on Ash by his eldest brother. Ash dislikes Ren on sight, but as the years pass and the two come to understand each other, his feelings for Ren gradually morph into something more. However, Ren shows no sign of reciprocating those feelings—and as Ash's recklessness leads him into danger, the truth may come too late.

Truth in the Wind
Copyright © 2020 Diana Waters
ISBN: 978-1-4874-2854-9
Cover art by Martine Jardin

Published by eXtasy Books Inc or
Devine Destinies, an imprint of eXtasy Books Inc

Look for us online at:
www.eXtasybooks.com or www.devinedestinies.com

TRUTH IN THE WIND
WILD MAGICS BOOK 3

BY

DIANA WATERS

DEDICATION

To Tim, my steadfast beta reader, and to Christina, who's been upgraded to Master of Horse.

PART ONE

CHAPTER ONE

"Breathe. Remember, your emotions should aid but never control you, or you will lose control of your Gift in turn. You must direct your feelings, not only your will, if you wish to master it."

Ash sighed, weary of hearing the same thing yet again. Still, he attempted to curb his growing exasperation and tried once more to send a gust of wind through the air to blow the stubbornly motionless scrap of parchment off the chair that stood facing him.

Nothing. The air was still, and he was all too relieved when his lesson was interrupted by a knock at the door.

"Mara. My apologies for the intrusion." Lelande—usually a stickler for manners—still had his riding cloak on. Ash peered at him curiously.

"Not at all, my lord. We were nearly finished for the morning—but who is this?"

Lelande stepped to the side, motioning to a figure standing behind him whom Ash had failed to notice until now.

"Ash, Mara, this is Ren."

Ash's eyes narrowed in suspicion. Sure enough, Lelande cleared his throat and glanced toward him.

"He is to be Ash's new . . . companion, starting from today. Ren, this is Mara, who has been a part of our household for many years as our instructor and resident herbalist. And this is my youngest brother, Ash."

Ash ignored the introduction. "You mean he's to be my bodyguard." He barely spared a look for the pale blank-faced boy standing mutely at Lelande's side, glaring instead at his brother with all the withering scorn a ten-year-old boy could muster.

Lelande turned to Mara. "Perhaps you could excuse us for the moment. I think I had best speak with my brother alone."

"Of course." Mara smiled and patted Ash on the shoulder before leaving the room, closing the door behind her.

An awkward silence followed before Lelande continued as though there had been no break in the conversation between them. "I judged *companion* to be the better term, as the former seemed so much to your disliking."

"I don't need a bodyguard. Or a so-called companion." Ash was adamant.

"So you say. But as it was either that or confine you to your chambers, posting a guard at your door day and night, I thought this to be the kinder option—for both our sakes. Now, pray, stop being rude and introduce yourself properly."

Ash let the silence drag out a moment, just to make it perfectly clear he still thought no better of Lelande's decision than he had several days ago, before finally looking at Ren again. "Ash Woodhart," he said, still glaring.

"Well met, my lord."

Ren's tone was deferential, his expression bland. Ash looked him over and was not impressed—mostly because if his brother was going to force a bodyguard on him no matter his objections, he had at least expected someone more bodyguard-like.

He had envisioned somebody large and intimidating, a man heavily muscled and bristling with weapons, perhaps even with a great prickly beard like the famed mercenaries he had heard of from far to the east. Yet this boy—and he was, unmistakably, a boy—stood several inches shorter than Ash himself. To add insult to injury, even if there had been a single weapon in sight, Ash doubted Ren would have known how to wield it. Everything about him was neat, nondescript and entirely non-threatening, from his plain dark riding clothes to his cropped brown hair with not a strand out of place. Even his eyes were closer to gray than blue.

Ash already knew he was going to dislike him.

"I thought you said bodyguard, not playmate." He turned his glare back to Lelande. "No offense to little Ren here, but I'm pretty sure I'd be the one getting *him* out of trouble."

"Would you have preferred to be followed about by a full-grown warrior rather than someone closer to you in age?" Lelande's tone was mild in the face of Ash's obvious disdain. "At the very least, I'll rest better knowing you won't be clambering about the mountainside alone from now on." His gaze lingered over Ash's tangled hair before moving pointedly down to his arms, bare below the elbow, taking in the dozen fresh scuffs and scratches amid the two dozen old ones. "Incidentally, you might keep in mind that *little* Ren here is a full two summers older than you, and in many matters far more experienced. Indeed, I believe you could learn much from him."

Ash scowled and rolled the sleeves of his shirt back down—a habit for which he was frequently being reprimanded. He was constantly being told it was not befitting for a gentleman to push up his sleeves—not even when it was very hot outside. "I can take care of myself just fine. Just because my Gift—"

Lelande held up a hand, forestalling his brother's protest. "Rest assured, your Gift has nothing to do with it. This is not a punishment, Ash. I am simply thinking of your safety."

That his last words were probably true did nothing to assuage Ash's temper. "So I'm to be followed around for the rest of my life then?" The thought of having his personal space permanently invaded by anyone, least of all this whey-faced boy, was intolerable.

"You'll have your privacy. Ren is to have his own bed-chamber, and much of his time will be occupied in training with the men while you take your lessons. But in every other way, Ren is to be treated as a member of this family. You will accept his presence and allow him to accompany you wherever you may go outside this house. In this, you have no choice. After you come of age, I may rethink the matter." Lelande stared levelly at him. "Trouble finds you, Ash, even when you're not seeking it out, and your well-being is more important to me than your pride. So for my sake, if not for your own . . . please?"

Ash could tell his brother was serious, because Lelande was calm and self-possessed and rarely begged for anything. He was begging now.

Ash turned his scowl to the floor. "Fine," he snapped with ill grace. "I'll put up with it." *For now.* "But it doesn't mean I have to like it."

Lelande sighed but did not scold Ash for his rudeness. "I suppose that's the best I'll get from you for the time being." He turned to the boy still standing beside him. "Ren, if you have need of anything, I will be speaking with Luck in the stables. My brother will see to it that you're shown around the manor. Isn't that right, Ash?" He waited for Ash's reluctant nod of agreement before turning to leave, and then Ash was left alone with the still silent Ren.

Ren looked at him. Ash looked back. The silence stretched out.

"Come on then," he huffed when it became painfully clear that Ren would not speak for himself. "I'll show you around."

"Yes, my lord."

Ash was already leaving the room before Ren had opened his mouth to reply. He walked quickly, forcing Ren to scamper to catch up. "And don't call me that," he added impatiently, not looking behind him. "My name is Ash."

"Yes, my lord."

Ash resented Ren, not just because he hated the idea of a so-called companion being forced upon him, but because he resented the bigger intrusion into his life, his home, his family. And the Woodharts were a close-knit family — grown closer still with the recent deaths of their parents — who annoyed and cherished one another in equal measures.

The oldest, Lelande, was tall and broad-shouldered. Calm and collected in all but the most trying of circumstances, his bearing was all that a lord of such a long-standing family should have been — though his temper, on the occasion he lost it, was quietly terrifying. Ash thought it was lucky Lelande had such strong shoulders, for he now bore the weight of responsibility for their house and their name upon them.

Then there was a big gap, because of the war, and so his two younger brothers had been born a full eleven summers later. Koresh was slender and graceful, his features finer than Lelande's, though he had the same forest-green eyes that had been passed down to all of them by their mother. His temper was quick as Lelande's was even, though in his fits of anger he rarely said anything he truly meant, and everybody knew it. He was born only a day before Ash — hours, really — but still liked to act as though he were Ash's senior by several years.

Ash tried to compare himself as little as possible to either of his brothers, for he felt any comparison was bound to be unfavorable. His hair was a disheveled mess no matter how many times he or anyone else attempted to tame it, his skin darkened immediately in the sun, and his clothes simply refused to stay clean or in good repair, even when he thought he was being careful. More to the point — at least as far as Ash was concerned — each of his brothers had mastery over their Gifts. To them, it seemed to come as naturally as breathing, while his own Gift, despite being the same in ability, was as fickle and capricious as the wind that was supposed to be at his command.

Aria was still a baby, the only girl and doted on by everyone. She had, against all odds, survived beyond the birthing chamber where their mother had not, and would likely come to look much like her in the years to come. Because of this and because Aria was such a sweet thing, with her easy giggles and tiny hands reaching eagerly out to explore the world, it was impossible not to love her. Determined to make her life a contented one, her three brothers spoiled her shamelessly, willingly taking on the roles of mother and father, sibling, and friend.

Even the servants that made up the rest of their far-flung country estate were as much a part of their home as anyone. Many of them had been a part of the household for years, like their parents and grandparents before them. A few, like Luck the stablemaster, had come from afar. Most others, like Mara, whose own hands had helped bring the four siblings into the world, had been around longer than anyone could remember. They rarely bowed or curtseyed unless guests were in residence, and Ash had grown up knowing all of them by name.

All mourned alongside the family after the loss of Ash's mother, who had been as kind and strong as she was beautiful, and for his father who wasted away after her in his grief. It was a sad time, but also one in which every member of the house stood united in their sorrow.

And into this comfortably familiar household came Ren— a near-mute boy whom Ash had never met—who, at Lelande's insistence, now followed him about like a second shadow.

This seemed a deeply personal blow to Ash, who loved his family but had an equally strong love for the freedom of his surroundings. Whenever Lelande became too irritatingly calm or Koresh too quick to vent his frustrations, Ash would escape into the hills, losing himself among the steep inclines and close-growing trees. There the mists rose from freshly dampened soil and gurgling rivers even in high summer, and Ash was a Woodhart through and through. Their home was rarely encroached by the outside world, for it lay deep in the southern countryside, where the Woodharts had bred some of the most sought-after horses in the kingdom since time immemorial. Their manor house lay in a natural bowl carved out by the sheer mountains on either side, and if Ash stood at its center and looked up, it felt like the Earth itself was cupping him in its hands.

Ren was a distraction Ash neither needed nor desired. And so while Ash was by nature neither cruel nor spiteful, he took every opportunity to try and leave Ren behind. He tolerated the boy only in that he never explicitly ordered him from his presence, but otherwise attempted to slip away at every turn, leaving Ren to chase after Ash wherever he might go.

At this, Ren proved infuriatingly skilled. Just when Ash finally thought himself free, and was happily scrambling up trees or digging in the dirt for treasure, there Ren would appear as if by magic, silent and watchful. Wherever Ash wandered the thickly-wooded mountains, jumping over rocks or roving among the forest, sometimes collecting herbs for Mara but usually simply adventuring alone, Ren would eventually track him down. It was as though he had some kind of sixth sense where Ash was involved. Like a shadow, Ren refused to be shaken, and Ash wanted to hate him for it.

Ash consoled himself with the thought that Ren would eventually tire of following around a constantly disappearing boy and would beg Lelande for permission to return home. No matter how hard he might try, he would never truly be a part of the household. He was an invader, an outsider, and while Lelande might ask Ash to treat him as a friend, there were some things quite beyond Ren's understanding. What more other than begrudging tolerance, Ash asked himself, could the boy possibly expect?

"Well, what did you expect?" Luck said, rolling his eyes.

Ash shrugged moodily. He liked Luck, who had a jagged scar over his left eye, the curliest hair Ash had ever seen, and a way of talking that never seemed patronizing or overly polite. On the contrary, there was a sardonic twist to his mouth that made every grin feel almost mocking, like he was secretly looking down on everyone for being who they were but at the same time couldn't quite blame them for it. It was said that Luck had fought in the war and been as lucky as his namesake to come out alive, though Ash had never asked him about this outright. There was a lot he didn't know about Luck, but the man had an easy way about him and wasn't afraid to treat him as an equal. Luck had always seemed like a kindly, if somewhat sharp-tongued uncle more than any kind of servant.

"I at least expected him to stop calling me *my lord* after the first few weeks," Ash groused. "It's not as though I act the part."

"Can't argue with that," Luck replied, not missing a beat.

Ash glared at him a moment, then gave a reluctant grin. "All right, so I don't act anything like a lord at all. Maybe I'll start wearing fancy clothes and ordering people about when you stop yelling at me about sitting properly and making me oil my own leathers."

"Can't help it if you don't sit right in the saddle, now can I?" Luck said, unconcerned. "And you have a perfectly fine pair of hands. It's only right a boy your age care for your own tack. Gods know most nobles wouldn't know how if their life depended on it." The scorn in his voice was evident, as it was every time he happened to mention the capital or the aristocracy residing there. "Save such ignorance for the castle lords—a Woodhart should know better."

Ash thought about grumbling some more but knew Luck was right. He gave his horse, a beautiful dark filly, one final pat and moved onto the next, beginning to detangle the lighter mare's windblown mane. Dusk was falling and they were alone in the stables, most of the other servants already retired for the day. Ash was not obliged to help, but it seemed only fair since he wanted to talk to Luck anyway, and the stablemaster still had work to do. The silence as they went about their work was a comfortable one, broken only by the sounds of stomping hooves, swishing tails, and the odd contented snort.

"So," Ash prompted again after a moment, "as you're the one who brought him here, you of all people should know. Why does he have to be so stupidly polite all the time? I've asked him to call me Ash and he won't. I've asked him to stop jumping to attention and bowing every time I so much as walk into a room and he won't. I've tried asking him questions and all I get in return are one-word answers, or a *such things wouldn't interest you, my lord*." He mocked Ren's color-less tone. "It's like trying to make conversation with a tree, only worse, because at least I wouldn't expect a tree to answer back."

"Boy's from the capital," Luck grunted as he inspected the hoof of a dun-colored gelding, as though that answered everything.

"So? You're from the capital and you still know how to carry a conversation."

Luck shook his head impatiently. "It's different there. You wouldn't know how much. People care more, much more, about the way servants speak—or should I say don't speak—to their masters for a start."

"Well, I'm not his master. And Ren isn't in the capital

anymore, he's *here*. If he really wants to be polite, then he should start acting like it."

"Half-Blood, too."

"What?"

"Ren. He's of mixed birth, same as I am."

"And how do you know something like that when he'll barely say two words to me?"

"Because I'm the one who arranged to bring him here in the first place, idiot. And because I knew his father."

Luck's gaze had turned contemplative. Ash stared at him a moment, struck dumb by his next thought. "Luck, are you..?"

"What?"

"You know . . ." Ash made an inarticulate gesture.

Luck stared at him before bursting into startled laughter. "The boy's father? No! Gods, no. You really *are* an idiot, aren't you?"

"Thanks," Ash scowled.

Still chortling, Luck replaced the pick he was holding and picked up a brush. "Sorry. Just the thought . . . but no. I knew his father from way back, before the war. We fought together, him and me." His smile faded. "Not the same man afterward, though. Well, and I suppose none of us were who came back out of there, but he . . . that was different."

Ash waited, but Luck didn't seem inclined to add anything more, and he knew there were some questions the stablemaster would flatly refuse to answer. Luck was talkative enough when it came to just about any other subject, but he didn't like to speak of the war and didn't take kindly to people prying. Ash returned to the subject at hand.

"So tell me then. Why should it matter if his father's from Iskandir?"

"His father's father, actually — not that such things matter in the capital, of course," Luck sniffed, continuing his brushing, and Ash listened over the chomps and stamps coming from the other animals, the rhythmic sound of Luck's brush cleaning the dirt and dust from the horse he was tending. "Look, things are different down here in the south. We're about as far away from the capital as it's possible to get from anywhere in the kingdom, and words like *Half-Blood* are just plain fact around these parts. Most people don't much care one way or the other, and even if they do, they usually have enough sense to mind their own business. They've got more important things to worry about. But the capital is full of nobles with too much time on their hands and not enough sense to saddle their own horses. Up there, those facts are names and the names are slights, and that's where Ren spent his whole life before he came here. It's all he knew. This may be his home now, but he's used to keeping himself to himself, and I can't say I blame him."

Ash still failed to see the problem. "It can't be as serious as all that, surely. The war ended over ten years ago, it's not as if—"

"Ash, you're a fine boy, but you don't know the first thing about it," Luck said flatly. "You weren't around then so there's no way you could know what it meant to be called Half-Blood, but I'm telling you, it was definitely *serious*. And a lot of people died for it, in the end." His words were matter-of-fact and there was no real anger in his voice, but his expression had turned grim, remembering. The scar stood out white from the rest of his sun-roughened face. "Ten years is like nothing in the capital. Nothing at all. I'm not saying it's anywhere near as bad now as it once was, mind, not by a long way, but laws are different from people. One of them can change from one day to the next, but the other takes a damn sight longer than ten years."

Luck looked as though he might say more, but then he only shook his head, as if to banish the thought from his mind.

There was another long moment of quiet as they continued to work.

"I'm sorry," Ash said, once he had judged it long enough to speak again. "I didn't mean . . ."

"I know you didn't." Luck looked at him, and his face wasn't grim anymore, but the smile he offered was not quite his usual teasing one either. "Like I said, you couldn't know what it was like back then. All this started and ended before you came into this world. Before Ren, too, but people are shaped by the others around them, and his father saw an awful lot. He never did manage to let it go afterward. Point is, the boy might need more than just a few weeks to get used to the idea that the way things are done here aren't like elsewhere in the kingdom. And if he never wants to talk about it, well, then it's his right to keep quiet—just like you got things you'd rather not speak on, eh?"

Ash took a moment to digest this, carefully not thinking about his father or, still worse, his mother. His hands felt suddenly cold.

He reached up to rub his horse's nose, glad for the breath and movement of something warm and alive tickling his skin. "Do you think he ever will? Speak about it, I mean?"

"Who knows?" Luck scrubbed a hand through his wiry curls, still a mud-dark brown with only a hint of gray. "Could be the more important question is, will you have stuck around to listen when he does?"

CHAPTER TWO

The weeks and months passed, and it was as though a kind of unspoken truce developed between them. Ash stopped trying to ask Ren personal questions and didn't try too hard to lose him in the woods — usually.

For his part, Ren seemed to at least make an effort to stop saying *my lord* every other sentence — though it seemed it was still beyond him to call Ash by name. Once in a while, he even offered up small tidbits of information about himself.

These instances were rare, and only ever seemed to happen whenever he and Ash were alone. Ash thought this odd, since if Ren felt close to anyone, should it not be Luck, who had brought him here? Or Lelande, who had allowed Luck to bring Ren? Still, Ash knew enough not to question it. Nor did he really mind the fact that in order to gain anything resembling personal information from Ren, he always seemed to have to give up something about himself first. It seemed only fair.

Mostly it was small things, like the fact that he didn't really care for reading but took pleasure in hearing stories spoken aloud, or pointing out the tree he'd fallen out of a year earlier and very nearly broken his arm in the process. In return, Ren told him, hesitantly as though embarrassed, that he did like reading but could only do so very slowly, and that he'd never broken his arm but had once broken several fingers when an older boy from the capital had challenged him to a wrestling match.

Indeed, sometimes there was little to do but talk, since

heavy rains in the winter made it too dangerous to venture outside, often for days on end. Flooding was common and the rain could make higher ground unstable. As lessons for Ash usually only took place in the morning, it was only too easy to run out of things to keep him occupied for so long. Koresh claimed he had now outgrown such games as hide and seek, while Aria could not yet reliably count to ten, let alone be counted upon to hide quietly herself. Ash had long since given up trying to play it with Ren, who was adept at hiding but somehow always managed to find his charge in record time.

Ash sighed, pressing his nose against one of the glass windows upstairs. It had now been raining almost without pause for three days, and his earlier restlessness at being cooped up inside had given way to a strange pensiveness.

"It was cold like this."

He didn't know what made him say it. Perhaps he was just tired of Ren sitting silent beside him, expressionless as always. Anything to prove that Ren was capable of feeling *something*.

"Cold enough to see our breath the day she died, even though summer had barely passed. We didn't know she . . . we knew Mother was ill, my brothers and I, but we didn't think she was about to leave us. If Father did, he didn't tell us."

Ash wasn't sure what he'd expected, but it hadn't been for Ren to nod like he understood. A husky sound emerged from Ren's mouth, before he cleared his throat and tried again.

"My mother too. But the baby didn't live."

Ash stared.

Ren looked away. "It's all right, my lord. It was a long time ago."

Ash wanted badly to ask what Ren's home had been like, if his father had raised him alone after that, if he ached sometimes for his mother in the same way Ash did for his own. But Luck's words came back to him and he held his tongue, hoping Ren would decide to say more.

If he was disappointed when Ren did not, he was at least not surprised. Even so, Ash continued, realizing that he owed Ren something more in return for offering up this knowledge.

"A healer came. Everyone already knew the birth would be hard. Father said women didn't usually give birth at that age at all. So Luck said he would ask an old friend to help. They came very early in the morning, before the sun had even fully risen. They must have been traveling all night." His words were halting, though Ash didn't mean them to be. "Two men, a blind healer and someone else—his bodyguard, I think. He carried a sword, at least. I never knew their names. But I remember the bodyguard had red hair, dark red, like . . ." *Blood.* He didn't say it.

Next to him, looking out the window, even though there was nothing there to see, Ren was silent.

"Even so, they came too late," Ash forced himself to continue. "We were outside the birthing chamber, my brothers and me. We heard Ari first and thought it was all right. Then we saw inside. There was . . ."

Ren turned his head back to glance at him, still quiet.

Ash swallowed, remembering. "She'd lost too much blood for anyone to be able to save her, not even the best healer in the kingdom. That's what Mara told us later, after . . ."

Ren's expression did not change, but he placed a hand briefly on Ash's shoulder—a rare gesture. Outside of his training, he usually touched nothing and no one, least of all Ash.

"I'm sorry," he said simply, and there was something in his eyes Ash could not name.

No longer trusting his voice, Ash jerked a nod and looked away.

15

Such raw moments of honesty between them were few and far between, for despite these occasional instances, Ren still seemed mostly averse to revealing anything about himself, no matter how small or insignificant. Ash therefore resigned himself to learning what he could from waiting and watching.

He learned that while Ren rarely smiled, and indeed seemed hardly to possess a sense of humor at all, he liked animals and implicitly trusted Luck. He was eager to help in the stables even when his training did not require it. Indeed, when one of the estate's several vagrant cats birthed a litter behind the hay bales, Ren could barely tear himself away. He never touched, as though he was afraid he might break the creatures simply by petting them, but his blue-gray eyes were wide and wondering, like he'd never seen such a thing in his life.

"Don't they have cats in the capital?" Ash asked him, rolling his eyes.

"Only ones that run away or hiss if you get too close. Not like this." Ren's voice was hushed, almost reverent, and it was enough of a change from his usual impassiveness that Ash could not bring himself to make fun of him further.

Other than this, Ren appeared perfectly content to sit and read for hours—perhaps because he had not seen many books before, either. While Ash busied himself outside, making tree forts and trying to catch fish with his hands, or playing with Aria and reading to her from storybooks, Ren would be a silently watchful presence somewhere nearby. By Ash's fourteenth year, having Ren follow him around felt almost as natural as breathing. If they were not exactly friends, then they were, as Lelande had once put it, companions. But fourteen was not an easy year for Ash—not because of Ren, but because of Amarillya.

Amarillya was Ash's betrothed, and had been since Ash's birth. Koresh would have been betrothed to her instead had he been born but a day later. Instead, Ash and Amarillya shared the same name day — a fact regarded as deeply auspicious, though Ash didn't care for tradition in the same way Amarillya's family seemed to, and he wasn't entirely sure that Lelande did either. Even so, it was not unusual for engagements between well-known families to take place from or sometimes even before birth, and Ash had given it little enough thought in previous years. Engagements could and were frequently broken with no party given offense. Even if they weren't, people could not marry until they came of age at fifteen, and often chose not to do so until much later.

Despite his disdain of old-fashioned customs, Ash liked Amarillya. She was undeniably pretty, with thick, glossy hair and clear blue eyes. She rode just as well as Ash did and danced markedly better. She could play the harp, too, and often allowed Ash to listen when he called on her at her family's manor.

Amarillya was, as the servants gossiped, *a proper lady*, but she never failed to speak her mind or voice her disagreement with Ash if she thought him wrong about something. It had been Amarillya who silently held one of his freezing hands between her own as he stood by his mother's funeral pyre, when his father, too distraught to pay much heed to his sons' distress, had been unable to comfort them himself, and Ash had never forgotten it.

Yet try as he might, Ash was never able to think of Amarillya in terms of marriage. She was his childhood friend and it seemed unnecessary for them to be anything more. He also thought it unfair that he, despite being the youngest son, was expected to marry when neither of his brothers had ever been engaged, nor showed any signs of being so.

In fact, Ash had never seen Lelande show so much as a flicker of interest in anyone, man or woman. He claimed he was far too busy to give a spouse the attention they would deserve, and Ash had to admit, there was probably some truth in this. When not overseeing the well-being of his younger siblings in some way, Lelande directed much of the surveying and work on their lands, allocated funds for necessary repairs and purchases of all who lived and labored upon it, arbitrated community disputes when others could not come to an agreement between themselves, and oversaw all their family's dealings with the buying, selling and breeding of horses. Even so, other lords appeared to manage just fine with their husbands or wives, whereas Lelande seemed utterly immune to any matchmaking attempts.

Meanwhile, nobody seemed to know what Koresh wanted — not even Koresh himself — although the topic made him cagey and snappish, especially whenever Ash happened to be present. "None of your business," was his usual answer to questions of that nature.

Ash wished he had the luxury of saying the same. He found his world suddenly changing now that he stood upon the brink of nominal adulthood, and as Amarillya began calling more and more often. He felt pressured by Lelande to likewise call upon her, now in the company of several maids or other servants, since it was no longer considered seemly for them to converse privately as they had done as children. This made Ash reticent, unwilling to speak his mind in the company of so many other listening ears. It also meant he was forced to think in practical terms about the future — one that he simply could not imagine spending together with Amarillya, no matter how much he liked or admired her.

And so, while at fourteen, Ash was expected to begin putting away such boyish pursuits as clambering the hillsides and exploring caves to spend more time at home, he could not quite bring himself to give up his freedom. The mist-shrouded mountains, the deep green of the forests, called to Ash more loudly than ever, offering him solace. He escaped among them now not to play, but simply to be alone — or as alone as Ash could be, with Ren ever at his side.

It was to the mountains he ran again the day his world changed a little more, though Ash would not recognize it as such until a long time afterward. On any other day, he might not have run off at all, for it was raining heavily, and early spring felt almost as cold as winter. But Ash's latest visit to Amarillya's estate early that morning was still fresh in his mind. They had gone riding before the rain could set in, and the way her fingers curled briefly around his own when he helped her onto her horse as he had been taught, the way her watching maidservant smirked knowingly, filled Ash with a sense of confusing disquiet. They talked only of inconsequential things, but Amarillya blushed when Ash remarked, as frank as always, that the bright red of her hair ribbons looked well on her.

"Do you suppose it might be a good color for a gown?" she had asked him. And then, without waiting for an answer: "I hear the ladies in the capital wear sleeves much wider than they do here. Perhaps I will ask Mother about it." Ash scratched his head, baffled. Amarillya always looked neat, her dress and bearing as composed as any noble lady from a great house, but had never before shown the slightest interest in fashion for its own sake. It made him feel as though there was something she was not telling him, or something important he had somehow overlooked.

Upon his return home, there had been yet another failure of a lesson with Mara. At first, Ash failed to raise so much as the slightest breeze to make the candle flicker, even though it was only a foot in front of him. Then he inadvertently summoned a wind with enough force to splinter both the candle and the legs of the table it stood upon. Seeing Ash's mounting irritation, Mara stopped telling him to direct with his mind instead of his arm and suggested they might want to pick up the lesson again another time, when Ash felt more *himself*.

Finally that day, there followed a loud argument with Koresh. Ash didn't even really know what they fought about, but his eventual anger resulted in an uncontrolled gust of air that sent a rare glass ornament toppling from a nearby cabinet. It shattered to tiny pieces on the floor, and Koresh glared. His final words before he stalked off stung bitterly, the glass in front of his feet parting as he sent a far more controlled draft of air downward to clear his way. "Better not to have been born Gifted at all if you cannot control your own abilities. Amarillya deserves better than the likes of *you*."

Suddenly the manor had seemed too small by half, and Ash knew he had to escape it before he started screaming from the closeness of it all, quite possibly bringing down the entire house upon them all in his frustration.

And so Ash strode, then ran, then sprinted, his breath bursting out heavy from his chest and the sound of his footfalls masked by the rain that had continued steadily all through the day. He slipped and almost fell several times, the dirt turned to slush and the dim light hiding tree roots in his path. His fine clothing was soaked through and spattered with muck by the time he finally stopped, the river roaring just ahead of him.

He approached the edge and simply watched a moment, unconcerned by the spray, since he was already hopelessly wet anyway. He let his breathing slow and his hands cease their trembling. The river was swollen from the rain and the recent thaw. It rushed and tumbled nearly as high as its surrounding banks. Staring at its ever-changing surface was oddly calming, and so by the time he turned around, unsurprised to see Ren standing silently just as though he had always been there, Ash did not feel like screaming anymore.

They stared at each other, Ren as quiet and watchful as ever, until Ash gave in with a sigh. "You should have stayed home," he said. "You didn't have to get wet, too. It's freezing out here."

"I know." Ren looked pale, but then, he always did. "We should go back."

"You can go back. I'm not ready."

"Then I will stay also, my lord."

Ash gave another sigh, this time more exasperated. "Of course you will." He turned away and began walking again, slowly now, further upstream. The water was too loud to hear Ren following, but Ash knew he was, and raised his voice so it could be heard above the noise of the river.

"It's not like I hate him, you know. He's just so . . . *insufferable* sometimes. But I expect you heard us fight."

"Yes." Ren was probably too polite to point out that likely everyone within several leagues had, though as usual, it was Koresh who had been loudest.

"Not that *that's* anything new," Ash continued, bitter now. "All we ever seem to do lately is fight. But it's none of his business about Amarillya. He should just marry her himself if he's so interested — gods know *I'm* not."

"Oh."

"Are you going to berate me too? Well, go ahead if you like. Tell me all about what a perfect lady she is, how pretty, how skilled at the harp, just like Lelande has a thousand times before. I already *know* all this, it doesn't make me want to marry her any more. Can't I like spending time with someone without wanting to marry them?"

"Yes."

"Just try telling Koresh that. I'm not—" Ash swore as he slipped, and thought he caught a low gasp from behind him, but he recovered his footing quickly. "I'm not saying I don't like her, but I don't *love* her, and I *know* it might sound like something out of a stupid children's story but I'm not going to marry someone I don't love. I'm just not." His tirade had left him breathless again.

"My lord, we should be going. It will be fully dark soon."

"I said I'm not ready." Ash stubbornly continued to walk.

"You'll catch cold, my lord."

"Or maybe *you* will. So if you want to leave then leave, but I'm not going anywhere."

"The banks aren't steady, my lord, you ought to move back."

"Oh, go *away!*" His anger burned bright again and Ash flung his arm out—not to strike Ren, but simply to punctuate his words.

The wind had been conspicuously absent before, for all the rain pelting down on them. Now, at his sharp gesture, it howled, shrill and ferocious—but not toward Ren. Instead, inexplicably, it forced Ash backward, one foot edging over the waterlogged riverbank.

He might have regained his balance if, right on cue, the ground had not given way from under his other foot. Ash flailed, trying to get back to safety, but it was too late to grab hold of anything as drenched earth crumbled away to nothing. He fell, the backdrop a blur of grays and browns.

"*Ash!*"

The splash his body made, the sudden, intense cold as Ash plunged into the river, drove all thought from his mind and all air from his lungs.

The water closed over his head, bubbling and rushing around him, but Ash was a strong swimmer. His head broke the surface a moment later, and he remembered he should be trying to kick off his boots and remove his jacket. It took longer than he thought, for his fingers were already growing numb and the current was relentless. It buffeted him this way and that, his body crashing into the bank several times, bruising him and making it more difficult to draw breath.

When he finally rid himself of the extra weight, he looked

up and found Ren, white-faced and shouting something at him that Ash couldn't make out above the roar of the water. He shook his head, hoping Ren would understand. Then he was being swept even faster downstream and there was no time to try and communicate anything more.

The world flew past him, and Ash desperately tried to grab hold of something—a stray tree root, an overhanging branch, a jagged piece of rock—anything to slow him down and give his hands enough purchase to haul himself from the water. What little he could find either broke away in his grip or was wrenched from him with the force of the current. He briefly glimpsed Ren again, running somewhere ahead of him and then jerking to a stop, dropping to the ground. For a moment Ash thought Ren was going to be stupid enough to jump in after him, but then he saw him shuffle forward on his knees and reach out a hand, and Ash realized he would have only a couple more seconds to try and grasp it.

He would have missed was it not for Ren leaning forward, far enough to fall into the river himself had his balance been any more precarious. Even so, the force of Ren's grip, the strength in his arm as he hauled Ash up and toward him when their hands locked, felt nearly enough to tear Ash's shoulder clean off.

Ash yelped in pain, Ren swore for the first time in Ash's hearing, and after a brief but terrifying struggle, they both found themselves on solid ground again, clothes dripping and chests heaving.

"R-Ren, you—"

"Shut up. My lord."

Ash snapped his mouth closed in surprise. He felt as though he should say something, but didn't know quite what. Ren was busy checking him over, possibly making sure he hadn't accidentally broken Ash's arm. Even if he wanted to, Ash found that he didn't have the energy to push him away.

His teeth chattered. "C-cold . . ."

"We need to get out of the rain, quickly. Now."

"If I c-can w-walk."

"You can't. Not for long, anyway. I'll carry you."

"A-all the w-way d-down there?"

Ren was silent, obviously thinking, and Ash tugged his arm.

"C-cave. Not f-far f-from here, r-rem-mber?"

A brisk nod. "All right. As fast as we can." Ren seemed to know the way once Ash had reminded him, but he wouldn't let go of Ash's arm.

Ash made no attempt to shake him off. They stumbled on, Ash's limbs half-frozen and clumsy, Ren grunting slightly as he began to take more and more of Ash's weight.

Had their destination been any further, Ren might well have been forced to carry Ash the rest of the way. By the time they finally collapsed inside the small cave, Ash could no longer feel his legs.

Ren took one look at him and began tugging off the rest of Ash's clothing.

"Hey . . ." Ash protested weakly as his shirt was wrestled from his shoulders.

"Your lips are blue. We have to get everything off before it makes you any colder."

"Oh." He wasn't shivering anymore, which seemed like a good thing to Ash, but Ren obviously didn't seem to think so. "How long are we staying here?" The thought, the words, were slow in coming.

"The whole night. It's too dangerous to go back down there in the dark with me carrying you the whole way, even if it wasn't raining."

"I can walk, if you just give me a minute . . ." Ash looked down and gave his legs an experimental wriggle, but his toes only curled and then relaxed again sluggishly. He gazed back up at Ren, grinning a little sheepishly, but Ren only frowned.

"You could too easily fall, or I could. If either of us were injured, we'd be trapped in the open and nobody would find us until morning." He looked Ash over. "Lie down."

Ren was already removing most of his own sodden clothing, and then he was quite suddenly bare-chested and easing himself down to the ground, making Ash do the same. The earth was not comfortable, but it was dry, and warmer than being outside. Ren's chest against Ash's back was damp but warmer still.

There was an odd sensation from further up his body, and it took Ash a moment to realize that Ren's fingers were burrowing through his hair. "What are you doing?"

"Checking for head wounds."

Ash searched for a reply, the words gradually coming to mind one by one. "It's too dark to see even if you felt any. Besides, what would you do if you found one?" His voice echoed slightly, and the sound of it bouncing from the walls made his head spin.

"Make sure you didn't fall asleep."

"I didn't hit my head that hard."

"You can't know that."

"Neither can you," Ash said, not caring that it was a roundabout argument. Not caring about anything much, beyond the fact that it was apparently impossible to wriggle any further back into Ren's chest. It felt reassuringly solid.

"Shut up," said Ren for the second time that day—and since it cost too much effort for Ash to keep arguing, he did.

If he eventually fell asleep like that, skin against bare skin, then Ren must have decided to let him after all, for Ash did not hear another word pass his lips the rest of the night.

On the outside, what passed between the two of them that day at the river, and the following night pressed together for warmth, amounted to little. Ash had been stupid and, he knew, entirely responsible for what had occurred. Ren had just been doing what he no doubt considered his duty. The only real outcome to speak of was Ash developing a hacking cough and both of them receiving a severe dressing down from Lelande, which Ash was well aware he richly deserved and Ren did not — though the older boy made no mention of this to anyone. If Ren knew that it had been Ash's unruly Gift that had caused the accident, he breathed not a word about it.

And yet, somehow, it changed everything. Ash couldn't explain his sudden fixation for someone who had already been by his side for four years. He kept watching Ren from the window every chance he got, and constantly thought about him whenever watching was impossible.

Almost as soon as he'd arrived at the manor those years ago, Ren had started training with the older men, whose job it was to safeguard the estate and surrounding countryside. While Ash attended lessons in the morning, usually with a tutor in one of the upstairs rooms overlooking the courtyard, or with Mara and sometimes Koresh in a spare room, Ren received his own kind of lessons. He worked on his horsemanship with Luck, learned woodcraft from the huntsmen, and practiced weapons drills and hand-to-hand combat with the guards. It had long become habit for Ash to glance from his books to the window whenever he was upstairs, from where he would often see Ren sparring with grown men more than twice his size, a look of fierce concentration on his normally impassive features.

This had been going on nearly every day of his life for years, yet Ash now found the routine inexplicably fascinating. Ren never saw him watching — he was far too focused on his training to ever catch Ash's eye — but now not a morning went by when Ash did not look for him. He had never particularly enjoyed being cooped up studying, since it was time he could have otherwise spent freely outdoors, but he began anticipating his lessons if he knew it would mean catching a glimpse of Ren, who was safely oblivious to Ash's stares.

As spring moved into summer and the days lengthened and heated, Ash found himself growing more and more interested by the sight of Ren. Or perhaps *interested* wasn't quite the right word. *Impatient* might have summed it up better, because it often felt like Ash was being forced to wait for something, even if he couldn't quite put his finger on what exactly that might be. Even Koresh, who Ash felt was hardly in a position to comment, noted more than once that Ash seemed oddly on edge.

Ash found it difficult to refute this. He couldn't seem to stop tapping his foot, brushing his hair from his face, shifting awkwardly in his chair every other minute. He once glanced out the window in the exact moment one of the guards must have cracked some joke or other, because all the men were suddenly laughing. Ash's gaze was instinctively drawn to Ren. Seeing him was like falling into the river all over again. Ash was suddenly unable to breathe. Ren's grin transformed his face, lit him up from the inside, and in that moment, Ash would have given anything to see that smile directed at him. *Anything at all.*

Then he recalled that for this to happen, Ren would actually have to be looking at Ash, which meant Ren would have to know that Ash was looking at *him*. At that thought, Ash had to abruptly leave the room, mumbling something about water. *Preferably to pour over my head rather than drink, but nobody else has to know it.*

It was also around this time that Ash's dreams became markedly more distinct.

Ash never had cause to feel embarrassed by his dreams before—not even the hazy, entirely pleasant ones that left him warm and shivery at the same time. Sex was not something he had ever been taught to be ashamed of—in the remote countryside, where horse breeding and farming were at the very heart of their domain, there was little point in being prudish. Ash had once happened upon a pair of stablehands behind a disused farm building, one man's muscular form stripped bare and his hair tumbling loose from its bindings as another moved rhythmically behind him, their hands braced together on the wall. They did not notice Ash. Although a little embarrassed at the sight, the incident had not bothered him unduly. Sex was simply a part of life, and one he had been acquainted with at least in theory since childhood.

Yet where Ash's dreams had previously been vague things, leaving him with only fuzzy impressions that rarely preyed on him by day, they now grew more vivid and entirely unambiguous. Where Ash had once abstractedly imagined graceful lines and soft curves, blurred faces with silkily trailing hair, now he saw — and felt, and touched, and was touched by — hard weight and solid muscle pinning him down, almost forceful enough to bruise, work-roughened fingers roaming his flesh, a mouth that took possession of his own and smothered his cries. A calloused hand around his cock.

He awoke to sweat-dampened sheets, and sometimes damp hands or thighs and stomach as well, and then he would purposefully remember the dream all over again and touch himself in earnest, and use the pillow to mask the guttural sounds emerging from his throat.

Those dreams were fervid and feverish, and left Ash with such an acute feeling of embarrassment that he could hardly bring himself to look anyone in the eye for hours afterward.

Ren remained, as always, unruffled and unreadable, and Ash tried desperately to pretend for both their sakes that nothing had changed.

CHAPTER THREE

Ash and Koresh's fifteenth name day celebration was a lavish affair. Half age-old ceremony, half boisterous festivity, it took place upon the Woodhart estate and was attended by a swarm of people. There were of course Ash and Amarillya's family members — not only those immediately related but also distant aunts, uncles, and cousins from both in and outside the domain — but many friends of the family came too, a few of whom had traveled from as far away as the capital and were provided guest rooms in the manor.

The music and dancing stretched out long into the evening. Between them, the two families had hired artisans to decorate the manor and estate grounds, musicians and entertainers to liven the festivities, and a large number of cooks and other servants to ensure the main evening feast would set tongues wagging in approval for days afterward. Name days were usually not quite so extravagant, but a fifteenth name day was special, for it marked the coming of age for both men and women. This particular name day was doubly important, as it also marked the day that Ash, still betrothed to Amarillya, would be allowed to marry.

Most did not marry so young and there had been no date set for the wedding, but it was clear the topic was not far from anyone's mind. The days and weeks leading up to the night of the main feast were therefore bustling, guests and servants alike constantly coming and going, for such a celebration could not be planned and prepared in a few hours or even days.

For his part, Ash tried to avoid this flurry of activity. It made him uneasy, and Ren too was clearly not happy at so many strangers being about the manor. When not attending his own duties, he seemed happiest sticking close by Ash and evading any unnecessary attention. With his oldest brother busy overseeing preparations and Koresh strangely withdrawn, Aria seemed to be the only one truly excited for the upcoming festivities. She gushed about the new gown she would wear and the new relatives she would meet.

By the time the evening finally arrived, Ren was even quieter and paler than usual, and Ash was strung tight enough that he felt he might snap at any moment. If yet another self-assured cousin or matronly great-aunt asked him, with a sly wink or coy flutter of a fan, if the courtship leading up to the wedding would be more traditional or if Ash preferred things a little more *unconventional*, he might throw his wine cup at someone, costly decorative glass be damned.

To Ash's dismay, there was neither time nor place quiet enough to be alone with Amarillya. She looked truly beautiful this night, her gown a deep rose color and the sleeves, he noted, wide and trailing. Her dark hair was coiled and held in place by a myriad of delicately-wrought jeweled pins, which sparkled in the light of the lamps and torches like stars.

Ash desperately wanted to speak with her, if only to finally ask if she was really as happy as she appeared or if she, too, just wanted to be left alone and not asked about marriage—*preferably ever*—but the opportunity never arrived. Everyone was too busy loudly congratulating them, or drinking toasts, or discussing plans as if Ash or Amarillya weren't sitting right there in front of them, like they didn't have a say in their own futures.

They exchanged wine, Amarillya smiling and giving nothing away, Ash feeling apprehensive and unable to speak much more than meaningless sentiment, try as he might to express himself properly to her. *Have we not been friends since childhood, always speaking to one another with honesty?*

"You . . . your gown is lovely." *Curse it, when did this become so awkward?*

"Thank you." She sipped the goblet he handed her, and her fingers were pale and elegant on the glass. The wine made her lips redder. He couldn't not look at them as she handed him a goblet in return. "You are handsome as well, Ash, whether you would believe it or no."

"I . . . yes. I mean no. I mean —"

"It's all right. You'll see." Over her shoulder, her father was looking at them both approvingly, and though she did not look at him, her lips curved wryly upward. "I'll not let my parents bully you into wearing anything you don't want to, when . . ."

"Are you sure?" Ash blurted stupidly.

Amarillya did laugh then, no doubt assuming he was still referring to the clothes. She placed a hand on his knee, beneath the table where nobody would see. The touch was more kind than intimate, a calming gesture. "Nothing has changed. You are still the same boy I've known since long ago. And I am still the same girl. No need to be so nervous."

"I know, it's just . . . I'm not —" They were interrupted by a cheer as the music began again and a troupe of dancers darted into the light in front of the tables, the moment lost.

Ash's discomfort did not wane as the celebrations continued. It was not helped by Koresh, who spent much of the night inexplicably glaring at Ash from his place on the opposite side of the enormous dinner table. Ash supposed his brother was jealous that he was not getting the same amount of attention, since it was supposed to be as much his celebration as it was Ash's. The only difference was that Ash was betrothed, though he could not see this as being in any way a good thing.

Aria, somehow sensing the tension between them, gave up

being petted and cooed over by the older guests to sit beside first Koresh, then Ash. Her excitement at all this—her first real feast, her first real gown—did not prevent her from drawing Ash's head down and bestowing a solemn, somewhat sticky kiss on his cheek.

"Don't worry," she told him disarmingly. Her mouth was still stained with fruit juices, but her wide green eyes looked wiser than any child of five summers had any right to be. "Even if everything else changes, I will keep you safe." She fell asleep against him a while later and was eventually carried to bed, happily worn out by the festivities.

Still the wine continued to flow as the families and other guests chattered among themselves. Ash found no further help from any quarter. Ren was a near-mute figure nearby, watching the event unfold without expression as usual. Even Lelande was of no assistance. Ever the practical man in the face of duty, Leland was fully occupied ensuring he carried out his responsibilities as host to the last. This included an enviable display of his Gift, which he used to send lighted candles dancing through the air around him in a kind of juggling act. The flames held miraculously steady even as the candles themselves flipped and whirled, drawing admiring exclamations from the guests.

The closest Ash got to voicing his uncertainties was when Lelande came up to clap Ash on the shoulder and ask if he was enjoying himself. He had, his brother noted, been rather quiet.

"I'm . . . I don't know if this is what I want." It was hard to make himself heard over the noise of the ongoing celebration. A fire breather had replaced the group of jugglers, drawing gasps and wild applause from many of the now drunken audience.

Lelande guided Ash away a little, to a table strewn with mostly empty goblets and the remains of the savory dishes.

"We all worry about such things when we are young." Lelande smiled wryly. "And when we grow older, too. But many of these worries fade in time. You'll see."

The wine that had been constantly pressed upon him throughout the evening made it difficult to voice what he wanted. Still, Ash tried. "No, I mean I *really* don't know. Please, Lelande. Can't we just . . . slow down? I don't need all this, I never wanted . . . I'm not ready to . . ."

Lelande understood then, though he seemed more kindly amused than concerned. "Rest assured, we're not hurrying into a wedding. Nobody is about to marry you off against your wishes like a sacrificial princess."

"I . . ." This was only half the problem, which Lelande, just like everyone else, clearly failed to realize. He didn't want to marry Amarillya in a year, or two, or three. He didn't want to marry Amarillya at all. *How can nobody else see this? How can Amarillya herself just be going along with it?*

"Ash." Lelande was serious now. "You are only fifteen summers. Feelings of affection, of love, take time. Allow some to pass before making up your mind. This is of great importance to Amarillya's family, to her father especially. And you cannot be blind to the way she looks at you. Just as we will not rush into a wedding, neither will we rush out of one. Everything will unfold as it must, in time. I promise."

"But—" It was too late. Lelande was already turning away, ready to see to the needs of his guests once more, and Ash was left standing alone, surrounded by suddenly flickering candles as a wind that had not been present before picked up and then died down just as briefly. Then the overly warm night air closed in around him once more.

"What of my own happiness? Is that not of any importance?" The question, spoken to nobody, was left unanswered.

"You'll catch cold, my lord."

33

That was Ren's way of asking just what Ash was doing, sitting downstairs in the dark at such an hour and drinking wine straight from the bottle like a — *well, certainly not like a noble of an old and great house.* Ash was not particularly surprised that Ren had found him. If anything, his mysterious ability to know where Ash was at any given moment had only grown keener over the years.

Ash looked up blearily, his fingers clutching the neck of the bottle. "I don't feel cold. Anyway, it's still my name day. Sort of." In truth, he didn't know what the hour was, though that scarcely seemed to matter.

The house had finally grown silent, the guests having either departed or found a bed. Not even the servants were still about — given the lateness of the hour, Lelande had declared the rest of the cleaning might be left until the following morning. Exhausted but unable to rest himself, Ash had wandered downstairs again, where he picked at the food still left out, vaguely hungry and realizing he had eaten little during the festivities.

That was before he had come across a nearly full bottle of already-opened wine and decided it might help him sleep. He knew it would not be missed. Now here was Ren, interrupting the quiet, although Ash found he did not really mind.

"If I may, my lord." Ren sat without waiting for an answer, his back leaning against the wall as Ash's was.

"You want a drink?" Ash held out the now half-empty bottle, but Ren shook his head. "You sure? It's good."

"I dislike wine."

"Really? Why? It's good." *Had I said that already? No matter — it's the truth.*

In reply, Ren only tipped his head back so that it rested against the wall.

Ash shrugged. "Fine. More for me." He drank, the wine warm and a little bitter in his throat, making his lips tingle.

"Are you going to tell me what's bothering you?" Ren was still not looking at him.

"Do you actually want me to?" Ash challenged.

"Yes."

"Then say it again. Properly this time, so I can tell if you actually mean it."

It was too dark for Ash to make out Ren's exact expression, and his eyes looked almost colorless in the gloom as he turned his head. "Yes."

Ash fiddled with the bottle in his hands, the wine sloshing gently back and forth, uncomfortable now that Ren was watching him. *Where to even begin?*

" . . . Amarillya kissed me as I bid her good night." The words tumbled from his mouth and though Ash immediately wanted to call them back, it was too late to do so now.

Ren blinked. "Oh."

"*Oh.*" Ash snorted and took another swallow of wine. "I suppose I should have expected that, coming from you."

A tiny movement on Ren's face might have been a smile. "And was her kiss so repulsive as to drive you to drink, my lord?"

If there was a rare touch of sarcasm in Ren's words, Ash chose to ignore it. "I did nothing to invite it, if that's what you're asking." Another sip, smaller this time, because his hands were no longer as steady. "I overheard her mother speaking to another guest about wedding decorations. *She's* certainly not wasting any time."

"And is it . . ." Ren hesitated. "Is the idea so distasteful to you?"

"Distasteful?" Ash was surprised at the idea. "No." He looked down, trying to find the right words to explain. *How can I say that I like Amarillya, yet can't even conceive of marrying her? How can I say that it's not simply a matter of time, no matter what Lelande keeps suggesting?*

Ash strove to find the words to explain all this to Ren —

who, despite still being shorter than him, had at some point seemingly outgrown him. Ren's obvious maturity left Ash struggling to reconcile his memory of the boy he had first met with the reality of the man in front of him. At seventeen summers, Ren was indeed a child no longer, making Ash all too conscious of his own lack of grace, his awkwardly long limbs and gawky movements. Ren was all quiet strength and smooth efficiency. Though he would never be tall, his body was hard and compact, his every step a purposeful motion. It was like comparing a full-grown stallion with an ungainly colt. If Ash inhaled deeply, he knew he would smell wood and leather, earthy and deep.

Now it was his turn to look away. " . . . I would never be happy with Amarillya," Ash finally admitted into the dark. "Not ever. Not properly."

There was the real truth of the matter, and now Ren was the only one who knew it.

"It's just not possible, and nobody seems to understand it but me," he continued. And then, because the silence was pressing on him, making his head and even somehow his chest hurt, "Besides, if I married Amarillya then you'd probably have to find another idiot lordling to bodyguard."

He had meant it as a joke to lighten the mood after his earlier words, but Ren froze. One moment he had been only still, but the next he was motionless, his face no longer simply impassive but a tense mask.

"*No.*"

The word was not loud, but Ash started at the intensity with which it had been spoken. "I was only — "

"Please, my lord. Do not dismiss me."

"I wasn't going to." Ash was baffled, about to say something else when he caught Ren's gaze again, and whatever he had been going to say fled from his mind at the look on the other's face. It was only there only for a moment, gone again

36

in the space of a heartbeat, but the fear was unmistakable. The air was sharp with it.

"When you come of age."

"I — what?"

"The day we were introduced. Your brother said he would rethink my position here after you came of age."

"I don't remember —"

"I'm begging you, my lord."

Ash could not look away from him, from the way Ren was staring at him in return, unblinking and more intent than Ash had ever seen him.

"Please don't send me away."

"I won't." What else could he say in the face of such a request? For Ren was indeed begging him, and Ash's wine-addled mind did not know what to make of it.

"*Promise me.*"

"I promise!"

Ren caught his breath, then abruptly seemed to recall himself. He turned away again to stare at nothing, until Ash remembered he was still holding the wine bottle in a grip that was now too tight.

He cleared his throat. "Will you at least tell me why you want to stay here that much?" *With me?* He dared not risk saying this last out loud for fear that denial would follow. He could only hope, and pray it was not utter foolishness to do so.

Ren's voice, when it eventually came, was low and a little husky. "I'm . . . I've never had a family before. Not like yours. Not like this. It's . . . it's home."

"Luck told me once, years ago," Ash admitted. The words tripped from his tongue, slurring together a little. "He said this was your home now. That your father wasn't the same when he came back from the war."

Ren's head jerked up at this and moved again in a stiff nod.

Then he stood, still not quite looking at Ash, and his voice still came soft but clear, each word a deliberate note in the dark.

"My father drank himself to death." Ash did not resist when Ren reached down to pluck the bottle from numb fingers. "We should go back to bed."

He could only nod dumbly as Ren helped him from the floor, half-wondering if this was yet another of his strange dreams. Half-hoping it was, for even in his drunkenness, he did not know how he could face Ren come the morrow.

The morning dawned gray and cheerless. Ash's head threatened to split itself in two, but the manor still had guests and it would have been rude to remain in bed.

Outside in the hallway, distracted by the dryness of his mouth and the desperate urge to find somewhere private to retch, he all but collided with Ren, who looked just as reluctant to leave the safety of his own bedchamber.

"Oh . . . ah . . . good morning."

"Good day, my lord."

Is it only my imagination that Ren sounds even more remote than usual? Although the events of last night, after the celebrations, were hazy, Ash remembered enough to know that he had embarrassed himself, and quite possibly Ren, too.

I should apologize, even if Ren won't make that easy for me. Maybe after my head has cleared a little, we can speak together alone. Somewhere outdoors, perhaps, if the manor's still too crowded.

He looked at Ren properly, about to ask him, and frowned at the sight of his face. Ren was always pale—now he looked waxen.

Instinctively, Ash reached out a hand. "Are you all right? You're—"

His words faltered as Ren jerked away, evading his touch. "I'm fine. My lord. We should be getting downstairs."

"Yes, but . . . what . . ." Confused, Ash could only gape stupidly for a moment, but Ren said nothing more. His eyes seemed cold and empty.

Ash tried again. "You don't have to go downstairs if you don't want. It's expected of me, but not — "

"Not of me." The reply was sharp, almost angry, but Ren's expression was as blank as it had been in the early days, before they had come to understand one another better. Before Ash had come to know how deeply his own feelings ran. "This is not my family."

"I didn't mean . . ."

Ren's shoulders were stiff as he turned his back to Ash. "They will be waiting, my lord."

Then let them wait. It would have been churlish to say it, but Ash still felt bewildered and hurt by this sudden change, wondering what he had done to deserve Ren's disdain.

Ren was the only one to understand him now, for Ash had not spoken to anyone else so openly of his uneasiness about the future. Yet here he was, plainly so affronted by Ash's very presence that he would not allow even the smallest of physical gestures.

"I can bring you water if — "

"No." Ren looked as though he might be about to say something else, before abruptly changing his mind. He shunned Ash's gaze altogether. "You do not seem well either. I will escort you downstairs, my lord."

He was already walking ahead, not waiting for Ash to gain his wits enough to reply, pausing only at the top of the stairway until Ash finally scrambled to follow. Their footsteps echoed, overly loud in the quiet.

"I . . ." Ash swallowed what he had been about to say. Ren must be very angry with him indeed, he thought. *But there will be time to apologize later, surely, if Ren will not allow me to do so now. He can't hold a grudge indefinitely — not when we live under the same roof.* "Very well."

They did not look at each other after that as they went downstairs to bid their guests good morning. They did not speak at all, and the silence drew out between them until Ash could finally bear it no longer.

He fled back to his chambers as soon as he could without causing offense, not daring to glance back at Ren. He was too afraid of what he thought he might see — and even more afraid of what he might not.

PART TWO

CHAPTER ONE

For years now, Ash had thought of gray as a cool color. Gray was polite and non-assuming and self-contained. Gray was formal and reserved. Gray created distance.

Seated now in a bustling tavern and looking across at a man he had never met, *these* eyes inexplicably called Ash closer. They were gray, yes, but they were also warm and knowing and inviting. They promised things rather than denied them, pulled in instead of pushing away, and Ash could not help but stare.

The expression that went with them was just as different from the one to which he had become so accustomed. Ren's read as clearly as though it had been committed to ink upon parchment: *close, but no closer.* This man's whispered: *close, but not close enough,* and Ash found himself instinctively responding, his body tilting itself forward and his fingers and toes tingling. Even the tavern itself seemed suddenly warmer. Ash's neck felt hot, beads of sweat gathering at the base of his scalp.

He could not remember the last time he had felt like this. Certainly not around Ren, at least—not since that dreadful night following his fifteenth name day.

As time had gone on, Ash felt a growing gap between them. In the space of a single evening, they had seemed to drift apart, as inevitably yet unexplainably as just about everything else of significance that occurred in Ash's life. Every day that followed, despite his efforts, Ren continued to step away until finally, all that was left was a frozen silence, broken only by the occasional nod of acknowledgment or murmured *my lord* in response to Ash's overtures.

Ash might have gotten over the fact that Ren would never love him—eventually—but to have that same man treat him as a complete stranger while they lived under the same roof was far more painful, and for years, Ash had barely thought of anything else. Nor could he admit to his pain to anyone else, knowing that he was probably the one who had caused such a rift in the first place. Not even Amarillya's pointed questions at Ash's distraction, which had always compelled him to blunt honesty, could make him confess his own stupidity.

His one saving grace had been that Lelande, true to his word, had not forced the issue of marriage with Amarillya. Still, Ash had the distinct feeling that Lelande was waiting for something—something that Ash was unable to offer. Whether this had anything to do with Ren's extreme aloofness, Ash did not know, but bridging the gap between them now felt like a near-impossible task. Ren showed so little interest in Ash or his affairs.

Is there even any point in continuing to try?

Someone brushed past him as they walked by. Ash blinked as the noise of chairs scraping, tankards clanking, people talking and laughing jostled him back to awareness. Ren's voice was mixed in somewhere among them and Ash glanced reflexively around, feeling vaguely guilty. There he was, talking to the innkeeper near the bar, looking as neat and composed as always.

The other man with the gray eyes sitting at the next table saw Ash looking, and gave him a smile that somehow managed to convey both playfulness and sympathy. In the late afternoon, with the sun streaming through the window behind him, a yellow jewel in his left ear sparkled. "Tonight?" he mouthed, so softly that Ash thought he might have imagined it. Almost.

Ash's eyes widened, but Ren was already turning to walk

back to the table.

The other man quickly put his head down, keeping his voice quiet. "After dark. Just to talk. I'll be waiting outside."

Ash did not have the chance to respond, for Ren was now only a step or two away, and without looking back, the nameless man was abandoning his seat and retreating, leaving Ash alone once more.

"My lord?"

"Hm?" Ash found himself avoiding Ren's gaze. Guilt continued to gnaw at him, along with a desperate hope. Hope that when he met Ren's eyes next, they would finally be looking back at him in the way he had always wanted, and continued to want. A gaze with no gaping chasm, no invisible barrier forcing him back like an intruder.

"Is everything all right?"

He made himself look anyway. But Ren's eyes were the same as ever, and something inside Ash sagged in disappointment. It seemed that Ren would never try to get beyond that barrier. He would never allow Ash to move past it, instead holding Ash at arm's length, just as he had always done. And always *my lord*, never anything other than this now, no matter how many times Ash reminded him otherwise, even after all these years.

He was so tired of reminding.

Ash nodded, wondering if his smile mirrored the same careful blankness he saw in Ren's eyes. "Everything's fine," he said.

But if everything were fine, Ash would not have been lying in bed hours later and listening intently, trying to work out whether Ren had fallen asleep yet, questioning whether this meant he had finally given up on Ren for good. He would have no more nightly visions that left him desperate and gasping, aching and empty. No more equally desperate hope that someday, *someday*, his dreams would become a reality if only he waited long enough. No more anything.

Outside though, the night was breathing and waiting for *him*. Ash breathed with it and made an effort to slow the beat of his heart. Nervousness gripped him, but he could not push the earlier conversation in the tavern from his mind.

I shouldn't do this, he told himself. *I shouldn't betray Ren's trust, shouldn't act so carelessly, shouldn't give him cause to worry. But if Ren's asleep then he won't have to worry at all, will he?* Neither could Ash wait indefinitely, forever held in place by the tenuous hope that one day, Ren might actually see him as something more than a now entirely thankless duty.

The idea of that last was enough. The wood boarding was cool under his bare feet as Ash slipped from the bed, but his body felt even warmer than it had earlier, like a fire smoldering beneath his skin. He moved slowly as he dressed, taking care to keep his breathing low and even, the whisper of his clothes just another natural sound of the night. The door lay only a few steps away, then the stairs, and beyond them the promise of something far more.

He turned to stare at Ren before he drew the door closed again behind him, still torn. If Ren woke now and questioned him, Ash knew he would tell him everything. He would admit how reckless he was being.

I'd beg Ren's forgiveness, and then — and then Ren would finally realize how I truly felt, put his hand to my cheek, tilt my head up, and Ren's mouth would —

No. And then tomorrow we would ride back home as though nothing had happened, because that's just who Ren is, and because the fact that I love him would not change a thing. Gods, but I'm so sick of trying and failing to make Ren actually see me.

But Ren did not wake—did not make so much as a single movement as a full minute dragged by. There was a soft click as Ash eased the door shut.

There was also pain, ebbing and flowing with each step

away from their shared room he took, but now Ash allowed curiosity and a bubbling sense of excitement to rise up along with it, pushing the other emotions back.

Just to talk.

He could not have explained aloud why he felt a thrill of anticipation run through him when he thought about who he was about to meet. The man had been handsome, true enough, but so were many men, and for the most part, it had not been his appearance that gave Ash pause. Nonetheless, Ash felt something unnameable course through him, making his palms grow slightly damp and his breath quicken.

The stairs creaked underfoot, but nobody was about. The tavern had closed its business for the night, the tables wiped clean, only the upstairs bedchambers occupied by drowsing guests.

When Ash stepped outside, the air prickled over bared skin where he had rolled his shirt sleeves up. He thought at first that nobody was there, either. The moon was bright enough to afford a view of an empty path lined by trees on either side, but nothing more.

He bit back his disappointment. Either he had left it too late or simply been given up on. More likely the latter. He was not appealing enough, not interesting enough, there was nothing about him that should attract—

"Here at last. I thought you might have changed your mind."

Ash started. The man had emerged seemingly from nowhere, this mysterious person with the eyes so like, and yet so blessedly unlike, Ren's. He was much taller than Ren, too, and even in the dimness, Ash could tell he had pleasantly sunbrowned skin. He must be used to being out of doors then, although he was not dressed like a farmer or any manner of servant. A wealthy merchant, perhaps, judging by the quality of his clothes and the flashes of jewelry.

"No, I just . . . it took me a while to, uh . . ."

"Ah. Under someone else's keen watch, perhaps?"

Reluctantly, Ash nodded. "He's asleep now. He wouldn't . . . I mean, he would have . . . I just needed to get out for a while."

The man's face was the very picture of understanding. "Of course. We all have our own troubles, our own private difficulties, and I would not dream of intruding on yours. But forgive my manners. Allow me to introduce myself properly. My name is Osias. At your service, my lord." He sketched a quick bow, not too low.

"I'm . . . ah . . ." Ash faltered again. It wasn't as though he was here in secret, and he was sure that the third son of a noble house, albeit a very old one, would be of little interest. *Still, should I really be blurting out my name to all and sundry?* He could see Ren in his mind all too easily, imagine his warning voice: *"You should take better care, my lord."* But *what good is Ren's advice now that I've already come this far?*

Osias spoke again as Ash dithered, before the silence could grow too uncomfortable. "No need to speak if you prefer to remain anonymous, my lord." He affected a teasing, conspiratorial whisper. "Many do, you know, for all *sorts* of reasons. Truly, I will not be offended. In fact, it only intrigues me further."

"It does?"

Osias grinned at Ash's surprise. His teeth were white and even. "Don't tell me you've never been an object of curiosity before. I'm only surprised you haven't already been stolen away, if I may be so bold. And I think I may." His eyes swept up and down Ash's body.

If there had been any subtlety in his words, there was none at all in his gaze, and Ash's excitement grew, half-recalled dreams crowding in his head — *held fast, fingers hard around his wrists, making him beg, a hot gaze burning him to his core —*

Ash felt himself flush, a heady mixture of embarrassment and pleasure sweeping over him at Osias' attention. "It's not like that," he managed to get out.

"No? Then I'm doubly glad we have such an opportunity." Before he had time to become any more self-conscious, Osias had taken Ash by the hand, gently tugging him to follow.

"W-wait, where are we going? I thought—"

"Relax—we won't go far. But we wouldn't want to wake anyone inside, now would we? It's very warm out, many of the windows will be open. The sound of our voices will carry."

"Yes, but—"

"Come, this way. Just a little further on so we won't bother anyone. I've no wish to be thrown out of yet another tavern." He winked, and Ash smiled uncertainly at what he thought must be a joke, allowing himself to be led on by the guiding hand at the small of his back.

Still, glancing back over his shoulder, seeing the tavern grow smaller and smaller behind him, Ash was sure Osias couldn't be leading him anywhere dangerous. Even so, he could not help but think that Ren would have never—

"Can we stop here? Please? It's just ... I mean, I'd rather not go any further until ..."

To his relief, Osias did as Ash bid. "Of course. I understand. See that little clearing over there? We can sit down for a while if you like. Get to know each other better." He smiled again. "Or if you like, I can do the talking and you the listening, since you prefer to remain such a beguiling mystery."

It was less a proper clearing and more simply a natural space between several large trees that grew huddled together, but it made more sense than standing about on the path. Osias leaned back against one of the trees casually, observing as Ash did the same.

"Shy one, aren't you?" he commented, watching as Ash tried to find a comfortable position, his eyes cast down.

"No ... that is, not usually. You remind me of someone,

that's all."

"Oh? Someone nice, I hope."

Ash was about to reply when he felt fingers on his arm, running up his shoulder and then cupping his face, tilting it upward.

"Wha—"

And just like that, Osias' lips were covering Ash's own. They sent an unexpected thrill down his back even as he broke away in shock.

"I thought—but you said—"

"I know. I'm sorry. But please, another moment only, I beg of you. Here, just let me—"

He drew Ash back in and kissed him again, this time not as gently. Still in a state of disbelief, Ash stood still and allowed it. Osias' mouth, his tongue, were alien and a little frightening to him, but Ash's body shivered from something that was not fear. His lips prickled and his chin angled upward of its own accord, even as Osias' fingers sought out his own and pressed against them insistently, pushing Ash's hands back against the bark of the tree—a not unpleasantly rough counterpoint to the smoothness of his lips.

Osias groaned something, gratifyingly breathless, briefly tightening his hold, then loosening it before Ash's thighs were unceremoniously pushed apart—

"Wait!" Ash jerked back with a gasp. "Stop, I don't . . ." But Osias moved his head down to kiss Ash's jaw instead, as if he had said nothing at all. Concern broke through the numerous other sensations that had begun bubbling up inside. "I said wait, I don't want—"

"No need to be coy with me." Osias spoke as if Ash were pretending, putting on a show of hard-to-get, and Ash began to struggle in earnest.

"Let go!"

"Oh, calm down, the way you were staring in the tavern,

practically begging me for it, it's not as if you didn't know—
"

Ash would have yelled if Osias' mouth hadn't claimed his own again, cutting off his protest and bearing down now with almost bruising force. Unable to free his hands, Ash panicked. As Osias' head inclined slightly, he did the only thing he could think of and bit down, hard.

Osias broke away, swiping at his mouth. "You little shit!"

"Let go of me!" Ash thrust himself forward, attempting to offset Osias' balance, but the grip on his wrists grew only tighter. Yelping as he was jerked roughly into Osias' arms and then shoved to the ground on his back, he opened his mouth to scream for help, only to realize the wind had been knocked from his chest. Silently choking and gasping for air, Ash could only thrash as fear took hold completely.

His movements were stilled when Osias used the weight of his body to trap Ash on his back, crushing him. Blood from Osias' lip dripped onto Ash's chin.

"I was going to take it slow, but it seems you have other ideas. Little slut."

Hands were at the collar of his shirt, wrenching it down and renting the material, Osias' voice sounding vehemently in his ear. Ash bent his knee and pushed up as hard as he could, but there was no room to land any real impact. He received a slap across the face for his efforts before Osias' knee once more forced Ash's legs apart, a hand fumbling at his hips.

Ash drew in another pained breath, pushing past the rawness of his throat, and finally managed a scream. The sound tore out of him, ragged and desperate, even as knuckles connected harshly with his cheek.

"Shut up!"

"Let go of me, let go—"

Teeth grazed at his neck, hands hard and vicious at his

shoulders. Unable to focus, weaponless, and with his Gift as always eluding him, he aimed another kick, this time connecting more solidly.

Osias grunted. "You'll pay for that, you —" His words twisted into a shriek of pain, and Ash found his body suddenly freed.

Clumsily, feeling dizzy and reeling with panic, Ash shoved himself up to his knees and jerked upright, preparing to flee.

The sight of someone forcing Osias to the ground and drawing a dagger to his neck stopped Ash in his tracks.

The point of cold steel pressed hard against his flesh stopped Osias, too. "All right, all right, I didn't hurt him, just having a bit of fun like he wanted —" His head was lifted and slammed to the ground.

"I am going to kill you." The voice that emerged from the other figure was Ren's, but Ash barely recognized it, low and feral with something that went beyond mere anger.

Osias blinked, seemingly disorientated from the blow, his response sluggish. "I won't do it again, I swear —"

"No. You won't." Ren's grip on the hilt of the knife looked painfully tight. His hand shook.

Osias gasped, his alarm obvious now. "I swear, I swear it, just let me go —"

Ren gave no answer and Osias fell silent. In the hush that followed, Ash could make out the panting from all three of them, hearing their different messages. Fear. Rage. Ash's own breath came in tattered gasps, almost sobbing in his shame and relief.

Ren turned his head at the sound, his white-knuckled grip not loosening. "Ash. Are you hurt? Did this man . . ." It was all too clear what he meant.

There was another loaded silence. Slowly, Ash shook his head. "No," he whispered. "I'm all right. Don't kill him, Ren. Please."

Ren turned back to his captive. The knife stayed where it was.

Ren's voice was now so low that Ash could barely make out the words, deliberate as each of them was. "If you ever think about touching him again. If I even catch sight of you, wherever you are, whatever you're doing. I will kill you." Nobody moved for a long moment as Ren stared into Osias' eyes, driving the message home. "It will not be quick." The knife was steady now, waiting. "Do you understand?"

Osias gave a jerky nod.

"*Say it.*"

"Yes, I understand, don't, yes, please—" The affirmation came rushed and garbled, but Ren moved his hand back anyway.

"Leave. *Now.*"

Osias bolted as soon as Ren lifted himself into a crouch. A crackling of branches heralded his flight before quiet eventually settled back over the clearing.

Ash was still trying to calm his breath when Ren leveled his gaze at him, and his knees buckled without warning. His face stung. He wanted to disappear.

He heard the soft crunching of leaves and the air shifted as Ren knelt in front of him. "Ash."

Wildly, Ash shook his head. He did not want to hear this—could not bear the thought of that terrible anger directed now at him.

"Ash, you're bleeding."

The unexpected softness of Ren's voice, however, was Ash's undoing. "It's not my blood," he said, a note of hysteria creeping into his voice.

Ren's eyes scanned the trickling wetness below Ash's mouth. His fingers moved to examine the swollen skin beneath Ash's right eye. Ash flinched away as something in him finally broke.

"Don't touch—" he managed to choke out, but Ren was holding him anyway, and Ash did not have the strength it would have taken to push him away.

CHAPTER TWO

Ash remembered little about their return to the tavern. Mutely, he followed behind Ren, staring at his back. It was straight and unyielding, and Ash wondered if he would ever be able to look at Ren again without seeing anger reflected back at him. He knew he would not blame Ren if this was so.

Already though, the events of the last few minutes were becoming surreal, as though they had happened to somebody else or occurred in a dream. *It's just shock*, he told himself. *You are not yourself yet.* But he did not know if he would ever truly be himself again—did not know if he even wanted to be. A numbness was flooding through his body, like his limbs were moving of someone else's accord while his real self floated somewhere beside him, watching all that went on in a kind of frozen detachment.

The tavern seemed very small when Ash entered the building again. He trailed Ren up the stairs, still silent, keeping his head down when Ren opened the door to their room and waited for Ash to go through first. He had not spoken a word since Ash's outburst. Perhaps, he thought, Ren did not trust himself to speak without shouting.

Ash sat on the bed while Ren lit several candles, sending shadows dancing up the walls, before rummaging through his travel pack. Turning back to Ash, he held a small linen cloth and an earthen pot in his hands. "My lord. I must examine your injuries now."

Back to *my lord* again, then. It seemed the only time Ren

was comfortable calling Ash by name was when his life was being threatened. In hindsight, that was probably a fairly obvious sign that Ren had no interest in him beyond obligation — no doubt just one of many such painfully obvious signs Ash had missed over the years.

Ren looked like he was waiting for his permission, so Ash simply nodded. He sat stone-still, hardly daring to breathe, as Ren knelt before him, angling his face gently toward the light.

Ash was glad there were no mirrors about, especially when Ren continued to hold his face still with the tips of his fingers as he wiped what Ash supposed was dried blood from his chin. He felt no pain, but had to make a concentrated effort not to jerk away when Ren opened the pot and began rubbing some sort of salve around the still-forming bruise under his right eye.

Ash stared past him at the wall. "Is it bad?" he made himself ask.

"It is not large, but will darken over the next few hours and probably swell a little."

Ren's voice was too calm, too neutral, and Ash wondered what was really going on behind those words. *Is he really seething inside, his rage carefully kept in check and simmering just below the surface? Does he just want to leave and never have anything more to do with me?* But there was no way Ash could ask these questions, too afraid of what the answers would be if Ren were honest with him. *And anyway, it would change nothing.* Lelande had charged Ren to look after his youngest brother, and Ren would obey as always, Ash thought.

"I need to remove your shirt."

"No." Ash's reply was instantaneous, the word spilling out before he realized he had even thought it.

"My lord, there will be other bruises from where you . . . fell. They need to be tended."

"They're nothing. I don't even feel them." It was true. Ash could not tell where the bruises were, if there were any at all.

The only real physical sensation he felt was his eyes, dry and itchy. He just wanted to lie down.

"My lord . . ."

"I'll check myself. Tomorrow."

" . . . Very well." Ren looked like he wanted to argue, but maybe he had simply had enough. Like Ash, he probably wanted only to rest so that the night would pass quickly and they could be on their way in the morning as soon as possible, leave and never come back to this godsforsaken place.

Ren got to his feet, secured the salve, and placed it back in his travel pack. "We'll leave first thing," he said.

Ash did not say anything.

He woke, or came back to awareness, to the sound of Ren readying himself for the morning. Ash guessed that Ren had not slept, although it was only the set of his shoulders, the slightly drawn look around his eyes, which gave him away. Ash himself had snatched a few moments of rest just before dawn and still felt dully tired.

Ren glanced over, seeing that he was awake. "We still have a little time, but my lord ought to dress while I see to things downstairs." He did not wait for a reply.

Ash scrambled out of bed as soon as Ren was gone. One of his shoulders now felt raw and throbbed insistently. He ignored it as he looked through his own pack for his second shirt. There was a small wooden washbasin by the table and a pitcher of water standing next to it, and he splashed cold water on his face — more in the hope that he would feel somehow cleaner than that it would shake him into sharper awareness. It did neither, and he made his way downstairs with feet that seemed to grow heavier with every step.

Ren was waiting for him by the door leading into the main public room. "There's food waiting for us."

"I'm not hungry."

"You must eat, my lord."

"I will. Later."

Ren looked him over, clearly wondering how far he should push.

" . . . I think you should eat now," he said finally. "Just a little will do. We'll leave straight afterward."

But the food, a thick, local porridge and a generous hunk of still-warm bread, stuck in Ash's throat, and after forcibly choking down a few mouthfuls of the breakfast that had been laid out for them, he could only push it around in his bowl. Perhaps he had gone suddenly white, because Ren got up to fetch him a mug of water without a word, pointedly watching as Ash emptied it.

"Ready?"

"Yes." Ash supposed he should resign himself to one-worded conversations with Ren from now on. He did not feel like talking, and Ren did not encourage him to, but it was clear that Ren bitterly regretted taking Ash with him on this journey.

At the time, Ash had seen it as an opportunity, and had all but begged Lelande to allow him to accompany Ren on his travels. It was the same horse market that took place twice every year in the outskirts of a neighboring domain—hardly an especially exciting or adventurous task. Nonetheless, various fantasies had filled Ash's head: that Ren had finally realized the depth of Ash's feelings for him, that Ren would reciprocate in kind and was using the journey as an excuse to do so, that they would elope to marry in secret and eventually travel back home, where Lelande would have no choice but to acknowledge their newfound sense of devotion for one another and give his blessing.

Looking back, Ash now saw that such thoughts had been not only naïve but ludicrous in the extreme. Ren had simply been being Ren, not thinking to protest Ash's idea of accompanying him to the market, taking Lelande's eventual, sighing assent as an order rather than a choice. After all, with Ren watching over him, what was the worst that could happen? What trouble could Ash possibly find for himself?

The horses were waiting for them once Ash had finally finished what food he could stomach, already freshly saddled and ready to carry their riders home, no doubt at Ren's efficient arrangements. He led Ash outside and secured their packs. "The weather is favorable. We should arrive back before nightfall."

They rode. Ren alternately walked and trotted his horse in silence, Ash following suit. Always, Ren kept just ahead and to the left of Ash, never quite looking at him, and Ash found he was grateful. It meant he never had to catch Ren's gaze even accidentally. It was not, he decided around mid-morning, that he was afraid of looking at Ren, but rather that he himself did not want to be looked at. The bruise under Ash's eye had swollen overnight, just as Ren had predicted, and he guessed it would now be impossible to miss.

Ash hated it. The pain, such as it was, did not trouble him, but the mark itself felt like a brand—a visible sign to the world of what he had done. As ridiculous as it would have sounded if he voiced the thought out loud, Ash felt that upon catching sight of it, all would immediately know how it had come to be there and who was at fault. He turned away from those they happened to pass on the road, even pulling up his hood to shadow his face, and was relieved whenever their path ahead remained empty.

Their journey, uninterrupted other than when Ren twice insisted on pausing to rest, passed by more quickly than Ash had thought it might. As always, Ren had been correct in his judgment, and they soon crossed back into Woodhart domain, arriving at the road leading to the main gate of the estate before the light had waned.

"Ren."

Ash had not intended to speak. The word had simply escaped his lips from where it had been sitting quietly in his chest for the whole day, waiting for an opportunity to free itself. Ren turned immediately in his saddle, and for the first time that day, they met each other's gaze. Ash saw no particular emotion in Ren's eyes, and did not know what it was Ren saw in return.

"Yes?"

"I was — there's something — "

Ren waited, holding his horse still.

"How did you know I needed you?" he finally blurted.

He did not need to explain his question further. "I heard," said Ren simply.

"But you weren't — "

"I was never asleep."

A wave of mortification swept over him. That meant that Ren . . . that all along, he had known Ash was going somewhere, had not tried to stop him . . .

"*Why?*"

Ren seemed to understand what Ash meant. "My job is to protect you, my lord. You are not my prisoner."

Ash wanted to vanish off the face of the earth. "You thought I wouldn't leave," he said, his voice blank with shock.

"I wanted you to make your own choice." Now it was Ren who was staring past Ash, seemingly unable to look him in the face.

Ahead of them, the outer gate to the estate loomed.

It was just their luck that Koresh was passing by as Ren first entered the manor, Ash close behind him.

His brother gaped for a moment, shot an accusatory look at the expressionless Ren, and grasped Ash by the shoulders, preventing his escape. "What in the name of all the gods . . ."

Ash flinched, but Koresh seemed not to notice. "This is . . . this is completely unspeakable, who would even dare to lay a hand—"

"I must first speak with his lordship." Ren's face might have been carved in stone.

"You will explain this to me, right now!" Koresh's fingers tightened.

"You're hurting him!"

Ash had never heard Ren raise his voice in anger before, and certainly he had never been anything but unfailingly polite to either of Ash's brothers.

Ash instinctively shrank back at the sound as Koresh finally released his grip, although this did not stop him from his interrogation. Demanding answers from both of them now, his voice grew louder and louder the more Ash refused to speak, his expression dark as a storm cloud.

It was not stubbornness that held Ash's tongue. Rather, he was no longer sure whether he was capable of speech at all. His final conversation with Ren seemed to have blocked his voice somehow, and he now felt oddly detached from the situation.

By the time Koresh had worked himself into a state of exasperated fury, there was one servant trying to make himself heard above the shouting and another standing shocked by the stairs while Ash stood silent, feeling unsteady on his feet. The room swayed vaguely about him.

"Koresh. Be silent." It was Lelande, striding through the entrance while removing his riding gloves, clearly having been occupied out of doors.

"But Ash is—"

"*Enough.*" The word was not shouted, but the tone immediately quieted everyone and everything within earshot, and Lelande seemed to take it all in with one swift glance—Ren's barely contained composure, Koresh's obvious anger, the servants hovering uncertainly nearby. His eyes flickered toward the other end of the room, and Ash saw with a jolt that Aria had appeared at some point amid the commotion. Her face showed an uncertainty that bordered on fear.

"Ash?" she asked, voice wobbling.

Lelande beckoned her forward, stooping down so that he was level with her. "Don't be scared, Ari. We're all fine, see?"

"But Ash, he's hurt—"

"Just a small accident, nothing for you to worry about. I'll take care of everything, I promise. Now, why don't you go and find Luck for me? I'm sure he mentioned needing your help today with the horses—I know he has some apples he was saving just for you to give to them."

Aria hesitated, glancing at Ash again, but Lelande gave her hair a tousle and nodded encouragingly, motioning for one of the servants to accompany her. "Go on now, Ari. We'll all be here when you get back."

He waited until she had gone before closing the outer doors firmly behind him and moving to stand behind Ash, one hand placed on his back in support. Into the silence, he issued several quiet commands that nobody dared disobey.

"Koresh, take Ash with you and go to Mara. She should be upstairs in her workroom. Do whatever she instructs—including taking your leave if she wishes to speak with Ash alone."

Koresh looked for a moment as though he might argue, but then only narrowed his eyes and took Ash by the arm.

"Ren." Lelande's face gave nothing away as he looked at the other man. "Accompany me to my office, now. Everyone else," and here Lelande raised his voice slightly so that any passersby, visible or not, would hear him, "should go about their business as usual. Anyone who refuses to do so will be facing my . . . extreme displeasure."

Not doubting his word, there was a general scramble as

people hurried to either make themselves scarce or follow Lelande's orders to the letter. Ash found himself being unceremoniously dragged off by Koresh, and although he wanted
above all to be left alone, he did not envy Ren's position in the
slightest.

Mara did not look surprised to see Ash when he appeared
with Koresh at his side. Doubtless she had heard for herself
the commotion downstairs. Still, she was calm as ever as she
looked Ash over, neither rushing to action nor passing judgment, her wrinkled hands sure and steady. The workroom
smelled of fresh herbs, sweet and earthy — lavender, valerian,
hazelmint, dragon's rue — among others Ash could not iden-
tify. He inhaled, his shoulders unconsciously relaxing a little,
making him realize how stiffly he had been holding himself.

"Be seated, Ash." Mara's words were not unkind, and her
easy manner soothed him further, her voice familiar to him as
that of any of his brothers. "Koresh, I think it best you leave
Ash to me. Run along now, dear." The endearment was affec-
tionate but firm.

Koresh did not argue — not after how clear Lelande had
made himself, though it was plain he did not like being dismissed. He gave one last scowl and left the room, flinging
back a hand to slam the door closed with a draft of wind for
good measure.

"Are you in any pain?" Mara asked once his footsteps had
faded off. She crossed the room to look over her array of me-
ticulously labeled jars and bottles.

Ash's voice was as husky as though he had not used it in
weeks. "No."

"That bruise on your face is not the only one."

"No."

"Hmm." Mara selected a jar, opening the lid to breathe in
the scent and nodding in approval. "This should do nicely, I
think." She turned to look back at Ash. "Have you used

anything already to bring down the swelling?"

"Ren . . ." His name hurt him to say. Ash swallowed past the lump in his throat. "He put some salve on the one on my face. Last night."

"Very well. Then please remove your shirt."

Fingers shaking, Ash did as he was told, and Mara examined the bruise spreading over his right shoulder. Her touch was gentle, and she said nothing to imply that she made any assumptions or blamed anyone at all for the marks decorating his flesh. But if the bruise on Ash's cheek was a brand, then he knew with a terrible certainty that the one marring his shoulder was unquestionable proof.

It was all his fault.

Several minutes later, Ash was dispatched briskly to his bedchamber. "Rest and quiet," Mara advised. "You should sleep if you can and eat later when your stomach settles. Drink some water in the meantime." Ash had not mentioned his faint nausea, but it did not surprise him that Mara somehow knew anyway. "I'll tell Lelande you're not to be disturbed."

Grateful for the excuse to avoid explanation or any further conversation, Ash left without argument, shutting the door to Mara's workroom softly behind him.

News traveled fast in the manor, and the place was quiet as he made his way to his bedchamber, the silence all but echoing from the walls. Turning a corner, he came close to bumping into Ren, who had been walking nearly soundlessly toward him.

Ash took one glance at his face and scurried onward, burning with shame. Ren had no need to say anything for Ash to understand exactly what had taken place in Lelande's study.

It was small and still in the midst of forming, flowering to life just beneath Ren's left eye rather than his right.

Otherwise, their bruises matched almost perfectly.

CHAPTER THREE

Returning to his bedchamber, Ash saw that someone had already placed a pitcher and glass as well as a large bowl of water on the bedside table, a dampened cloth draped over its side. He made sure the door was firmly shut, then stripped and washed away the dirt and dust gathered from the road, careful not to look down at his bruised shoulder. His body felt heavy and slow. He did not return downstairs that day, instead taking Mara's advice and retiring to bed early.

Even so, as the minutes turned into hours, the shadows growing longer as the last of the light dimmed, Ash felt wide awake. He could hear the creaks of the manor, the familiar squeaks and groans of doors and shutters, the quiet humming of a servant going about her work—all familiar noises that Ash found vaguely reassuring, but which did nothing to lull him to sleep. Even as exhaustion clawed at him, Ash could only stare at the ceiling, his eyes bone-dry and aching.

Ren hated him. Of this he was certain. If Ren had not before, he would have no alternative but to do so now. Ash had caused Lelande to strike out at Ren, as surely as if Ash had struck Ren himself. Whether Lelande considered it Ren's fault for not stopping Ash before events had been allowed to escalate, or whether he felt Ren had not done enough to reach Ash in time after the danger had become apparent, it made no difference now. Ash was fully aware that everything that occurred had been his own fault, from beginning to shameful end.

Ren's hatred was therefore entirely justified. Lelande's

contempt for Ren was not. *Ren must have reported what had come to pass in such a way as to make Lelande believe that it was not my fault, or else Lelande had simply misunderstood.* Ash knew his older brother, always cool in a crisis and no lover of violence, would never have struck Ren if this was not so.

As for Ash's own part in the situation . . . well. Lelande would never strike Ash, for even at his angriest, he would never lay a finger on his family. No, he would devise some alternative kind of punishment for Ash — something more appropriate given his bloodline and social position. Ash turned over the possibilities in his mind.

A year's worth of chores in the stables for Luck? But of course not, that would be too kind by far. A year spent in captivity, then? But likely it would be more suitable for Lelande to strip me of my name and send me into exile, since I've certainly tarnished the family's name as well as my own.

Not only that, Ash thought in a sudden flash of cold, but he had also incited Ren to threaten murder, which was surely a crime punishable by the crown. Perhaps Lelande would write to the queen, requesting Ash's royal detention. Public whipping. Permanent banishment from the kingdom.

As Ash waded through the ideas, each of them more horribly fitting than the last, he became fixated on the idea of his sentencing, whatever it was to be. Lelande was probably only taking pity on him, allowing Ash a final night of peace before announcing his just punishment, he thought.

But with every passing moment, Ash felt the guilt weighing him down further. He needed to know *now*, before the estate, then the whole domain, and finally the entire kingdom began to grumble at Ash's avoidance of his crimes. He needed his shame to be balanced out harshly, fairly, with a proper sentence. He needed Ren and only Ren to hate him, because if everyone else started hating him as well then Ash would not be able to bear another dawn in this place.

The more Ash thought these things, the truer they became,

and in the end, he could not wait — the urge to get up and find Lelande, to demand immediate condemnation of his actions, became overpowering.

Not bothering to change from his nightshirt, Ash slipped from his bedchamber, silent as a wraith. He wasn't sure where he would find Lelande, for his brother often stayed up well into the night writing or reading — sometimes in his study, sometimes in the library or in his own chambers — but Ash's feet led him through the door and down the hallway of their own accord.

Lit only by now guttering candles, the hallways twisted and warped about him, and Ash stumbled onward, as unable to stop walking as he had been to sleep. The motion dizzied him, so that it seemed hardly surprising when he bumped into the solid form of another person there in the dark.

"Who — Ren!"

"My lord." Ren's face remained in shadow, but his voice was unmistakable.

"Sorry, I'm sorry, I couldn't see . . . what are you doing here?" Ash did not recognize this part of the manor at all in the darkness, and it seemed strange that he should have found Ren in such a place purely by chance.

"Waiting for you, my lord. Ash."

That single word caused a thrill to reverberate through him, making his body tingle and his tongue trip over his reply. "For . . . for me? But I, but — Ren, how did you know? And why — "

"Just to talk," Ren interrupted, and although these words made him vaguely uneasy, Ash was given little chance to think about why, for Ren was already kissing him. Hungrily, possessively, as though Ren desired nothing more in the entire world but this and now. *Ren* was kissing *him*, and his hands touched Ash in a way that had him gasping and shuddering, melting into Ren's embrace and wanting more, *more* —

Ash. I've wanted you. I've always wanted you. Ren did not speak, not exactly, but Ash heard his voice resonate around them nonetheless and could only hold on tightly, his fingers digging into Ren's shoulders, as the air warped around them and they both toppled backward.

He felt little impact when they hit the floor, Ren's body still sheltering him in a strong embrace. The stone should have been cold beneath them but was only pleasantly cool, and anyway, when Ren kissed him again, his hands sliding under Ash's nightshirt, the floor could have been made of ice for all Ash cared.

Just to talk, Ash heard again. Chest tight, heart thumping loudly in his ears, Ash's eyes fluttered closed. His skin felt stretched, as though his desire was a physical thing that might escape his body. Dimly, as Ren leaned down to claim his mouth again, Ash answered aloud. "But we're not doing much talking at all."

Of course we are. Look again.

Ash opened his eyes once more, and his mouth opened too to form a scream. Under his very gaze, the shadow that was Ren was taking a different shape. Ren's eyes continued to stare out at him, but it was Osias' hands that now grasped his body. Tightening painfully, they bit and burned at his skin, branding him with a hundred more bruises, a thousand more blue-black smudges of shame.

You wanted this. You still do. You asked of it — asked of me.

"I didn't, I don't, let me go!" But Ash's voice was thin and powerless. He was not winded this time but still his voice had trailed away to nothing, gradually fading with each dying breath. The air was being squeezed from his body, he was being crushed under the heaviness of the lie. He knew it was his own fault, for who else's could it have been, but did he really deserve *this*?

Call for him. Call for Ren and we'll see what he makes of this, shamelessly moaning under the body of another man. Little slut.

The pain was crawling under his skin and rushing through his entire body, powerful as a river. It was all true. He didn't want Ren to see him, half-naked and thrashing beneath the one person who had already made him so angry.

Call him, let him watch you beg, and he'll tell you how he feels, how he truly *feels about you.*

Another precious breath was wasted on a feeble cry as the weight became too much to bear.

. . . him . . . call him . . . call him . . . call . . .

A stabbing in his head as the voice grew and echoed. Whether he wanted to call out to Ren or not, only a final, desperate whimper left his mouth with the last of the air in his chest.

"Ash!"

There came the faint sound of his name. He heard Aria's voice, wildly out of place with the rest of his surroundings. He struggled up and out in a blind flurry of clammy limbs and sweat-soaked hair, wild with panic. Koresh was yelling something in his ear but in that moment, Ash understood only that his shoulders were being held in a vice-like grip.

"*Let go of me!*"

His Gift, raw and potent, answered his terror, sending Aria's small body slamming against the wall.

Miraculously, although shaken, both Aria and Koresh escaped the situation without a scratch. Aria, hearing her brother groaning in his sleep, had gone to wake Koresh, and both siblings had entered Ash's bedchamber to see what was amiss. This Ash surmised from their explanations when things had finally calmed, after Lelande had rushed in, alerted by the noise, and Mara had come and gone — this time with a concoction to make Ash sleep more deeply.

Ash woke again the next day, his head groggy, the sun already long up. He dressed and went to find Lelande, who was bent over a stack of parchment in his study, his quill busily scratching.

While Ash was aware that his thoughts about due punishment the previous night had been addled, and for the most part completely ludicrous, he was sure Lelande would at least have a few choice words to say to him. Ash had not only done something indescribably stupid, putting himself at risk and getting Ren in trouble for it, but he had also come close to causing his own siblings real physical harm. Accident or not, it was a grave offense to use one's Gift directly against another. This was one of the core tenets of the very kingdom, and one that every child, Gifted or not, grew up learning. Ash had no excuse.

He knocked quietly at the door. "Good morning, Lelande," he said, when his brother kept his head down and made no move to speak.

"Good morning, Ash. You're feeling better, I hope." Lelande continued to work, only briefly glancing at him beyond the cordial greeting as Ash lingered in the doorway.

" . . . About last night . . ." Ash finally ventured.

Lelande did look up at that. "I had thought you might wish to discuss that later." There was no anger in his voice, but Ash fidgeted anyway. "Very well. Come in, sit down. I will be finished in a moment. Have you eaten?" Lelande gestured toward a plate half-filled with sliced fruits, nudging it gently toward Ash with a puff of air from his Gift before his quill returned to the parchment.

Ash sat but made no move to eat, his stomach churning uneasily. His back was stiff as he waited for the stern reprimand that was surely on its way, this time entirely deserved. As Lelande continued to write, Ash's gaze slid unwittingly to the window, from which a group of guards could be seen working through a series of weapons drills. Ren, his own back as straight and correct as ever, followed along in the exercises, his body moving fluidly through the motions.

If I'm to be sent away somewhere, will I at least be given the chance to apologize properly to Ren first? To speak with him, just one last time?

" . . . with Mara alone from now on."

Ash turned back as the last of Lelande's words sunk in. "What?" he asked blankly.

Lelande's brow furrowed further, no doubt at Ash's lack of attention. "As I was saying. I think it best that you and Mara practice control of your Gift without Koresh present. Perhaps somewhere out of doors, where you are less likely to be accidentally interrupted. Gods know Aria is growing more curious by the day — her nursemaid can't keep up with her. I hope Mara is up to the task of instructing one more, when it comes time to do so." He sighed, looking weary.

"Oh. Yes. Of course." Frankly, he was surprised this hadn't been suggested sooner. With as little control over his Gift as he apparently had, Ash was clearly a danger to anyone around him, even aside from his usual carelessness.

But this was not what he had come to Lelande about. Ash made an effort to sound calm, but the faint tremble in his voice betrayed him. "Please, just tell me. I have to know."

Lelande looked at him, puzzled. "Know what?"

"What my punishment is to be."

"For what?" Lelande was leaning forward now, his expression wary.

"For what I did to Ari. And for . . . for what I did before. When Ren and I . . . when we were away. I—"

He was too ashamed to continue but Lelande was already shaking his head, stopping him. "Nobody blames you for what occurred last night. It is a crime to use a Gift as a weapon, no more than that. And as nobody was hurt by it, I see no point in dwelling on the issue." He dismissed the matter with a wave of his hand. "As to the second, you must know that was not your fault."

"But it was. You don't understand, Ren didn't do anything, it was me who—"

71

"You are mistaken." Lelande's voice was suddenly chill. "It was precisely because Ren did nothing that you . . . that the events of that night were permitted to occur. Ren understands this very well."

"But Ren was . . . he couldn't have known, and I didn't see it either, I was so . . . but by then it was too late, and it can't have been Ren's fault no matter how you look at it because *I* was the one who — "

"No." Lelande stood, interrupting Ash's ramblings, and strode over to him. Ash stared up at his brother, lips pressed together against a rising current of distress. "This was not your fault," Lelande repeated firmly. "You should know that Ren has already provided me with a full explanation of what occurred. He knows just as well as I the folly of his actions. He put your life in jeopardy, and was then foolish enough to let your assailant go free after that person . . . after he *dared* . . ." Lelande turned quickly away, his fists briefly clenching, so that Ash could only guess at his expression.

"Lelande..?"

His brother took a deep breath, then another, before turning back to face him. "Ren let that man go," he finished more calmly, "when he knew very well what he should have done instead."

Ash jerked to his feet, unable to remain silent at Lelande's swift judgment. "But I told Ren not to do anything! He asked me and I *told* him — "

"It makes no difference! Were I in Ren's place, I would have torn that depraved beast limb from limb for what he tried to do to you!" Lelande's shout rang from the corners of the room.

Without realizing it, Ash had taken a step backward, his body now painfully tense. Seeing this, Lelande lowered his voice again and made a discernible effort to relax, but his words did not soften. "I would have killed him," he continued steadily. "And then I would have come back here and begged both forgiveness and punishment for my extreme lapse in duty, and for my failure to provide adequate protection."

This last startled Ash into agitated response. "Did he?"

Lelande bit back what he had been about to say at the stricken look Ash was unable to hide. " . . . Ren's punishment is yet to be decided," he replied carefully.

Ash shook his head. *Wrong. Wrong, it was all wrong.* I'm *the one who's meant to be punished,* I'm *the one who brought this on Ren . . .* He couldn't think, couldn't breathe, but the injustice of it all was bearing down on him and all he wanted to do now was leave. Run. Far enough away that he wouldn't hurt anyone ever again.

Unconsciously, Ash was backing away from Lelande and toward the door. He understood it all now, and the thought sent shocks of icy coldness through him. Why Lelande seemed so quick to blame Ren, and why nobody had already demanded Ash's punishment.

Gods. How could I have been so blind?

For Ash's own sake, to save him from the disgrace of what he had done, Ren had lied for him. He *hadn't* told Lelande everything, instead somehow making himself out to be the one responsible—as though Ash had not left the safety of the room that night of his own free will and for his own gratification, fully aware and intending of his actions.

"I . . . I don't . . . this isn't what I . . ."

"Ash!" Lelande's voice was sharp with concern and Ash met his gaze. Practical, reasonable, Lelande's eyes steadied him a little, bringing reality briefly back to a standstill. Still, Ash knew he could not stay here. Not in this room where, only hours ago, Lelande had struck Ren with a blow that should have been meant for someone else. Would have been, if Ren had told Lelande the truth and not taken Ash's own punishment on himself.

The truth was enough to make the bile rise in his throat,

and he looked at Lelande in despair.

"You don't understand," he said, and as the self-loathing welled up in him and finally overflowed, his Gift burst forth and the room erupted into chaos.

CHAPTER FOUR

Days passed by in a murky haze.

After the wind had finally died down, his Gift spent, which had mercifully not been long but still left Lelande's office in a state of utter disarray — parchment torn and scattered, books toppled, ink pots upended, glass smashed and even a heavy tapestry ripped from the wall — Ash had been sent firmly back to bed. Too exhausted to argue or make another ill-fated attempt at explaining himself properly, Ash eventually realized that Lelande would not have listened anyway. He would simply carry on insisting that it wasn't Ash's fault, laying the blame instead upon Ren.

The knowledge that nobody thought Ash responsible for his own actions made the days pass even more slowly, and he could not settle to anything. Small noises often made him jump, and the mere thought of eating made him feel physically ill. Ren no longer joined them for meals, and Ash forced the food down his throat only so that he would not cause any more trouble than he already had.

Because Ren, likely at Lelande's orders, had distanced himself completely from Ash and could now only be seen training alongside the other men-at-arms, Ash spent much of his time in his brother's watchful presence. Lelande need not have bothered keeping such a close eye on Ash — the forest did not tempt him, and he felt no inclination at all to run off on his own. His own home no longer felt safe, and Ash dutifully read or studied while the others went about his business. If Lelande noticed that Ash's attention was often elsewhere, he did not reprimand him for it.

Neither did he say anything of Ash's progress, or the complete lack of it, resulting from his extra lessons with Mara. Ash's Gift now failed to materialize at all, no matter how Mara instructed him to breathe or what to envision. Over and over, she advised him that self-doubt was his own worst enemy, to simply feel the truth of his power within him and then allow it to flow out. Over and over, Ash failed. Try as he might, not a puff of air from Ash's efforts stirred the blades of grass around them.

Koresh, whose temper had appreciably cooled over the past few days, tried talking to Ash. Although he clearly meant well, Ash was still quite unable to answer his questions, and could not face the idea of going out walking or riding with him. First Koresh was only quietly exasperated, then he grew angry, then he grew angrier. Finally, he gave up altogether, although Ash could see that beneath the bluster, he was hurt by Ash's silence.

Aria, meanwhile, asked no questions of Ash at all. Too young to understand even had anyone thought it appropriate to explain, yet old enough to know that something had caused a deep wound to her family, she kept him company for a part of each day, trying to comfort Ash in the only ways she knew how—singing the same lullabies he had once sung to her when she was a baby, reading to him from storybooks, sometimes crawling into his lap or slipping her hand into his without a word.

"I will keep you safe," she told him gravely, and while she was there, Ash could almost believe it.

Amarillya called at the manor at least twice that Ash was aware of. Both times he refused to see her, leaving first Lelande and then Koresh to make his excuses, knowing himself to be a coward. Even so, he could not bring himself to welcome any visitors, Amarillya least of all.

He glimpsed the second of these visits from indoors and watched from the window, unseen, as Koresh stood beside her, gesturing something, his bearing uncharacteristically awkward. If Amarillya felt distressed or discomfited in any way, she gave no sign of it that Ash could see, and soon rode away with her maidservants in tow.

Ash was not sorry to see her leave. If it was impossible to discuss with Koresh any of what had taken place, it was unimaginable doing the same with Amarillya, to whom for all intents and purposes, Ash was still betrothed. She was yet another person who Ash had thoughtlessly wronged by his actions, seeking out a dalliance when he still owed her his allegiance, and he could face neither her anger nor her forgiveness, whichever she chose to offer.

Proper rest, at least when darkness fell, became impossible. After two evenings spent tossing and turning, Ash gave up and kept the candles burning through the night, staring at the play of shadows on the walls. He caught up on his sleep during the day, and supposed the servants must have grown used to stumbling upon him curled up in a private corner of the library or snoring beneath a row of trees in one of the enclosed gardens. Occasionally he fell asleep inadvertently, whisked away by the security promised by sunlight and open space, only to wake some time later to find that somebody had placed a cushion under his head or a pitcher of water on a nearby table. This embarrassed him, as it meant he was failing to be anywhere near as discreet as he was trying to be. The fact that he never seemed to stir whenever anyone touched or tiptoed around him only compounded his unease.

The final blow was realized, inevitably, several days later when Ash awoke after one such accidental nap in Lelande's study. His eyes fluttered open and he sat up quickly, glad at least that he hadn't nodded off on top of the nearby pile of freshly-inked parchment. A hurried glance at Lelande told him that his brother had likely noticed but was tactfully keeping his mouth shut.

Ash cleared his throat self-consciously. "Sorry, Lelande. I guess I've been a little tired recently . . ."

"Only a little?"

Ash flushed. "It's just—it's difficult to sleep at night, just sometimes, so . . ."

Lelande looked as though he wished he could take back his words. Quite possibly, Ash thought, wincing, he was recalling what happened the last time Ash had gotten upset in his usually pristine office.

"I only meant that you should take care not to push yourself too hard."

You look terrible. Ash heard the unspoken words and looked away.

"I know. I'll be more careful." *Careful not to fall asleep in front of Lelande again, at least.* He turned his head to glance out the window.

The courtyard below was empty.

Ash's breath caught in his throat as his hands gave an involuntary clench. Nonetheless, he took pains to school his features into some sort of composure before turning back to Lelande. "Ren's usually out there this time of day," he mentioned in a tone he desperately hoped sounded nonchalant.

Lelande stared at him. "Ash . . ."

Ash's breathing quickened as he abandoned all pretense. "Where's Ren?"

"Ash, calm down and listen to me—"

"Just tell me." He was on his feet without knowing how he had come to be standing.

" . . . I thought you already knew," Lelande finally said into the ringing silence. "Ren's gone, Ash. He left this morning."

"What do you mean, gone? Left *where*?"

Lelande shook his head. "I don't know. He requested leave

for a time, as is his right. I granted it. His business now is his own. I do not pry into his private affairs."

"But *why*? How could you just let him leave like that?"

Lelande gave a heavy sigh. "Because I felt it was for the best."

His brother's forced air of calm grated on him. "What are you saying? That he's been dismissed from service? That you don't want him here anymore, with us? With me?"

"I did not dismiss him. Ren left of his own accord. He is a grown man capable of making his own decisions. Ash, I cannot claim to know how to solve everything, but all that I do is intended to be in your own best interest!" Pain was etched starkly in the lines on Lelande's forehead.

It was this, more than anything else, that broke through Ash's distress. " . . . I'm sorry. I didn't mean . . ."

Lelande passed a hand wearily over his face, and Ash saw the heaviness there, the weight of the burden his eldest brother was doing his best to carry alone.

"I'm sorry, too. For everything that's happened. I'm so very sorry."

Their positions had been reversed, and at any other time it might have been funny. "Please don't say that. It's not your fault, Lelande, I promise."

"If I had taken things more seriously, not tried to force the issue with you and Amarillya . . ."

Ash shook his head, caught off guard by Lelande's words. "I don't understand. What has any of this to do with Amarillya?"

"Oh, Ash." Lelande's expression showed exasperation mingled with pity.

"*Oh* what, what are you . . . oh. *Oh*." Realization dawned.

There seemed nothing more to say, certainly no way to argue. There was a moment of pained silence.

" . . . You know then," Ash said blankly.

"Yes."

"For how long?"

"Long enough." Lelande gave him a strained smile. "Since just after your fifteenth name day, I suppose."

"Then why didn't you say anything? Why does nobody ever *say* anything?"

"Because your feelings are your own," Lelande said, his voice now gentle. "And because nobody else has a right to know them until you are ready to speak. Ash . . . there's nothing wrong with falling in love."

"No. Just with betraying Ren's trust in me."

"You know I never meant—"

"I want to be alone. May I be excused? Please?"

He turned and left before Lelande could answer, desperate now for privacy, and Lelande did not call him back.

Ash's feet led him to the stables, where he remembered too late that hay was far scratchier than it looked.

He tried to ignore the way it itched—the stables were otherwise a near-perfect haven for an afternoon nap, just bright enough in the day that he felt safe, but also large and cool enough that he could find a comfortable corner out of sight behind the bales. Best of all was that, despite the steady stream of traffic in and out of the building, there was a distinct lack of gossip here.

Ash had borne the constant, albeit hushed chatter of the servants over the past weeks without a word, but only because speaking to anyone about it would have merely drawn more attention to himself. The stable boys, however, had no such time for chatter—or if they did, it did not revolve around people. In their domain, horses were their only concern—the growth of the colts, which of the matured males might be coaxed to mate with the fussy mare being kept in the meadow nearest the river, which animals would eventually fetch a high price, and which must be kept for breeding.

Nobody noticed Ash there in the hay other than the mother cat and her newest litter, none of whom paid him much attention. Their quiet mewling, the whickering of the horses, the business-like chatter of the stable hands washed over him, harmless and soothing, eventually comforting him enough to find sleep.

The long, hot weather continued unbroken as summer progressed, making Ash all the more thankful for his hiding place behind the stacks of hay until, several more days following his self-imposed isolation, he woke to a laidback whistling.

Warily, he raised his head to listen more carefully, the hay rustling underneath him at the movement.

"Awake now?"

Ash instinctively froze, then relaxed as his sleep-addled mind caught up with his senses. The question had been neither unfriendly nor confrontational, and Ash sat up fully, his head emerging from where it had been concealed behind the bales.

Luck was seated on a rickety stool that creaked when he moved, slowly and methodically oiling some horse leathers — a large pile of them, saddles and bridles both — in a heap beside him. He was not facing Ash.

"How did you know I was here?"

Luck shrugged, not pausing in his task. "These are my stables. It's my job to know all that goes on here. Must just about have a sixth sense for it by now."

"Oh." Ash watched the movement of Luck's shoulders as the man worked, unruly curls bobbing whenever he shifted position. Quiet descended again.

"Was there something you wanted?" Ash asked eventually, when Luck made no move to look at him or speak again.

"Not really. Some company, if you've a mind to help. But you can go back to sleep if you'd rather. I'll not be disturbing you—or telling anyone else you're here."

"No, I'm awake now. I'll help." The steady progression of rag against dry leather was oddly calming in its own way, and in any case, it was not in Ash's nature to look on as someone else worked right in front of him. Scrambling up, brushing stray wisps of hay from hair and clothing, he made his way over the top of the bales to where Luck was sitting, just inside the shade of the overhanging roof.

"Which one?"

"Take your pick." Luck paused in his task for a moment to indicate the pile of leathers. "Just grab that rag there and dip it into the oil—you'll see there's no great trick to it."

Ash quickly realized Luck was right. His muscles were aching satisfyingly after a few minutes, copying Luck's way of moving the rag in small outward circles from the edges of the leather. It was no difficult task, although Ash, who had not done any real physical work in some time, found himself tiring quickly. The sensation was not unpleasant—in fact, it stirred up a vague contentment after so much inactivity.

"So," said Luck conversationally. "Not sleeping so well lately, I take it."

There was no point in denying it, though Ash resented the comment all the same. "Did Lelande tell you to ask?" he said, and was a little taken aback at the bitterness he heard in his own voice.

"I've seen neither hide nor hair of his lordship all day," Luck replied, unruffled. Ash glanced at him a little suspiciously, but there was nothing in Luck's manner to indicate a lie. The stablemaster's hands continued to work at the bridle in his lap. "Doesn't take much smarts to figure it out, though. You leave the candles in your room burning, don't you? You can see the light from the stables, you know."

Ash was forced to concede the point, nodding reluctantly. "I don't like sleeping at night anymore," he found himself saying. "It's just . . . it's easier not to, that's all," he finished, flushing slightly.

"Fair enough," Luck shrugged. "Times were I didn't care for the dark either."

They continued to work companionably for a while before Ash finally asked a question of his own, feeling that Luck might actually listen.

"Luck, do you . . . do you know what happened?"

"Lelande told me what Ren told him, nothing more."

"You mean Ren didn't say anything to you himself?" Ash asked, surprised.

Luck shook his head. "Ren's always been one to keep personal matters to himself—never gives much away, that one, even to people he's known for years. But I expect you know that."

"Mm," Ash agreed. "I just thought . . . you know, since you've known him the longest, he might have said something."

Luck shook his head. "I knew his father. Good man, once. Just wanted the best for his boy. I never did know Ren before he came here, you know—not properly, anyway. Only ever met him a few times, and he was a quiet boy even then. But no. He's not said a word to me about it, and I don't expect him to."

"I see."

Another space of silence stretched out between them.

"Although something tells me," mentioned Luck offhandedly, several minutes later, as though no time at all had lapsed, "that Ren didn't quite tell Lelande everything."

Ash's hands immediately stilled. Luck still wasn't looking at him, but Ash knew he was waiting for something. For Ash to stop talking. To get up and walk away. To run.

Ash took a deep breath and did none of these. "What makes you say that?"

"Oh, no real reason. Just the feeling that it doesn't quite add up. Not like Ren to be so lax. He's always followed after you like his whole world depends on it." Luck shot a meaningful at Ash before continuing. "So it's not much of a guess that he left something out of his story —"

"He did," Ash admitted in a rush, and his voice shook. "I found out from Lelande, by accident, and that's why . . . but Lelande wouldn't listen and I couldn't tell him afterward because of what happened in his office and then Ren, he . . . he left . . ."

"Ash." Luck's voice was quiet but firm. "You do know Ren didn't leave because of anything you did, right?"

Ash shook his head. "You can't know — you don't know what I did . . ."

"I could take a guess. Put two and two together."

Ash's hands began to shake along with his words. "You can't have guessed, otherwise you would hate me too."

"Don't be daft," Luck scoffed. "Nobody has any reason to hate you. Ren of all people —"

"You can't know that!"

Luck took a moment to consider. "No," he said eventually, his words measured. "Don't suppose I can for sure. But if you really believe Ren could hate you, you don't know him anywhere near as well as you should."

His tone was not one of accusation, but Ash found that he could not stop the words now that they had begun to fall from his mouth, heavy and ugly and filled with all the guilt that had been stored up inside him until this moment. Waiting to be let out. Waiting until Ash might finally *explain* himself.

Like a dam bursting, the truth flooded out, rushing from the opening that Luck's casual manner, his non-threatening presence, had created.

A brief but sudden gust of wind punctuated his words. "He looked like him. He looked so much like Ren, had eyes just *like* his only he didn't push me away, he actually wanted — I waited for so long and Ren never so much as smiled at me, never called me anything but *my lord*, even though for months, for *years* I'd been — and I know I shouldn't have believed what he said, I know I shouldn't have gone out that night alone, it was so *stupid!* And afterward, even though I wanted Ren to yell at me and hate me for it, he never said a word, not a single one . . . and then when I learned what he'd told Lelande, that's when I knew Ren must really have come to hate me, because how couldn't he when I'd done such a terrible thing and made him take the blame for it? Luck, I miss him! I miss Ren so much, even though I don't have the right to, just like I wouldn't have had the right to stop him even if I knew he was leaving — " Ash choked to a stop, his ears ringing with regret.

Luck remained silent until the air had settled around them and Ash's breathing had slowed. "It doesn't matter. None of that changes anything. It wasn't your fault. You hear me?"

"But I — "

"You made a mistake, no doubt about that. But a mistake is all it was. Ash. You hear me?" Luck was looking at him steadily. "It's no crime to want . . . things, to desire things, from other men or women. It's not wrong and it doesn't give anyone else the right to make you think otherwise."

Ash's voice sank to nearly a whisper. "But what I wanted — he said I begged him for it, he said I was the one who — "

Luck's hand cut through the air, punctuating his words. "You're *not* to blame for what happened, Ash, no matter how much you've obviously been trying to convince yourself otherwise. If Ren knows anything about what happened, it's that."

"But that's just it, he doesn't know, I never told him — "

"Ren knows more than he lets on," Luck interrupted. "Come on, Ash, give the man some credit. He might not say much, but that doesn't mean he's ignorant."

Ash gave a laugh that sounded almost like a sob. "I do know that."

"Then you should also know that Ren left for his own reasons, not for the ones you've invented."

"Then *why?* Why did he leave without telling me? Before I could work up the courage to even speak to him again? Before I could tell him . . ." Ash was pleading, desperate, willing Luck to give him an answer he could believe.

But Luck only shook his head. "Can't answer that. Maybe he feels as guilty as you do. Maybe he just needed some time to clear his head, get some air. Gossiping servants around here, you know." That wrung a wobbly smile out of Ash, and Luck looked pleased.

"Luck . . . I want to believe that. I do. But Ren . . . he looked so angry that night, and I can't — I have to talk to him myself. And nobody knows where he went or when he'll be back. How do I know he'll come back at all, after I did something so . . . after everything that's happened?"

Luck looked at him as though Ash really was stupid then. "If he's angry at anyone still, it's at himself. I doubt he was ever angry at you to begin with. Besides, where else would Ren go, when you're still here? I already told you. This is his home, you mean everything to him. He's not one to give up so easy. Not after so many years."

This took a moment to sink in, and when it did, Ash felt his body burn with embarrassment. "What are you . . . did Lelande tell you — "

"No, you idiot. But it's as plain as day to anyone with a working pair of eyes. Now you just need to be patient. And while you're at it, you might think about how you can make it up to Ren, if you really think you've wronged him so badly."

"There's nothing I could do that would make it up to him,"

Ash said miserably.

"That's just not true and you know it. And even if it were, do you think Ren would want you to live like this for the rest of your life? Alone and afraid? Look, I've made my own share of mistakes. Said things, done things I'm not proud of, and plenty of them. Think I've never made a fool of myself before? That you're the only one in the history of mankind to screw up? Take it from me, the only thing for it now is to forgive yourself. Everything else—the apologies, trying to get things back to normal, whatever else—it can't come 'til later."

"How do you know that?" There was a speck, a fragment of something growing somewhere inside him. Like a tiny seed, it emerged from the dark, making him both excited and urgently afraid all at once.

Luck snorted. "I know a few things you don't." His tone turned reflective. "People hurt others around them. That's just the nature of the world. But they can bring happiness to others, too. Maybe not right away. Sometimes not even for years. But people can learn. Tell the truth, set things right. Even oblivious lordlings like yourself," he grinned, softening the insult.

"I . . ." Ash stood up, feeling somehow dazed as a thought struck him.

"You all right?"

"Yes, I . . . Luck, I have to go. I'm sorry, I need—I'll help with the oiling another time, okay?"

He barely took in Luck's nod before Ash was running, tearing across the grounds in his haste to be alone, to shield the idea lying vulnerable and still budding somewhere deep inside.

His heart pounded with terror at his audacity. Terror, and a wild hope. He was beginning to know now what it was he had to do, if only he had the dare to do it.

That night, when it was time to retire, Ash lit his

accustomed oil lamp and made his way not to his own bed-chamber, but instead to someone else's.

He fell asleep there, clutching his hope in his hand and breathing in the lingering scent of Ren.

Chapter Five

A sh's patience was stretched to its limits over the next few days. The sun rose and set and rose again, and still there was no sign of Ren.

He resisted the urge to steal out from the estate and find Ren himself after his conversation with Luck. His guilt, the sense that he had betrayed both Ren as well as his own feelings for him, was still churning about inside him, but this was now paired with a kind of urgency. It made him want to hurry and explain everything to Ren, to make it clear why he had acted the way he had. He wanted to apologize, to make Ren see that Ash accepted at least some responsibility for whatever Ren might be feeling and was ready to try again — to rebuild their relationship from the ground up, if that was what it took.

But no matter how much he wanted these things, he also knew that even if managed to sneak away without anyone stopping him, the likelihood of somehow stumbling upon Ren was almost non-existent. Nobody knew where had gone, and Ash would not have known where to even start looking. More importantly, assuming he managed to find Ren without getting into any trouble along the way, Ren would not be happy with him. To intentionally put himself in danger like that — to ride out alone, without anyone knowing where he had gone — would not be taken well by anyone, and he owed both Ren and his family better. No, Ash would simply have to wait, accepting that Ren would return when he was ready, on his own terms.

No matter how hard it was to believe, now was not the time for action, but for patience.

In a way, it was probably a good thing that Ren had not found his way back just yet, he thought. Ash fully intended to explain it all to Ren when he did, however painful and embarrassing that might be — but before he could do that with a clear conscience, he needed to talk to Amarillya. She deserved far more than Ash's silence.

Well acquainted with her family over the years, Ash was greeted with barely more than a raised eyebrow when he called on Amarillya without arranging their meeting ahead of time. As his horse and servant-groom were led to the stables, another servant led Ash upstairs and into an airy room overlooking the lakeside.

Ash could hear Amarillya before he saw her. She had always been skilled at the harp, and the sounds of the strings carrying through the hall were clear and precise, struck with no hesitation.

Her fingers paused and dropped to her lap as the servant guided Ash into the room, though she made no move to stand. The breeze through the open window stirred her hair and the folds of her gown as she gazed at him coolly. There was a brief, awkward silence, which not even the usually chatty maid who kept Amarillya company on a chair next to her looked inclined to fill.

"Amarillya . . . can we talk?"

She nodded stiffly. "Leave us, please," she said to her maid and the manservant still hovering nearby.

"My lady . . ." The maid looked uncertain even as she took the harp from Amarillya's hands. "It's not entirely proper —"

"Father will have already been informed of Ash's arrival, I am sure. He may come here himself if he sees fit."

The maid seemed about to argue, then apparently thought better of it at Amarillya's frown. She bobbed a curtsey and left, and the manservant bowed and closed the door behind them.

Amarillya looked at Ash silently another moment and then stood, smoothing her skirts as she walked to the window. She looked out at the lake.

"Well," she said eventually. "You've come here to talk. Talk, then."

"I suppose . . . I came here mostly to apologize. I hurt you by refusing to speak with you earlier, I know that. I wasn't thinking about your feelings when you came to visit . . . I wasn't thinking much about anything, or anyone. It was self-ish of me."

"Yes, it was." She glanced at him, and now there was anger in her eyes, if not yet in her voice.

Amarillya continued to look at him, silent and unblinking, and Ash knew she was waiting for something else. He shuffled his feet, knowing what he had to say yet reluctant to speak further, aware that it might well hurt Amarillya even more.

He struggled to find the right words — any words. "Amarillya . . ."

"Yes."

"About us," he tried awkwardly. "I don't think we . . . that is, I know we're not — that I can't —" Amarillya's glance moved away from him, and Ash knew he would need to do better.

"It's about Ren," he said abruptly, and felt himself grow red, not only in embarrassment but also shame that it had taken this long to tell her something he had known for years.

"No."

Ash thought she was denying his words at first, perhaps about to try and convince him that he was wrong, but she shook her head when he made to speak again, and now she was facing him fully.

"It's not *about* Ren at all. It *is* Ren."

As Ash gaped unintelligently, Amarillya raised an eyebrow. "Oh, don't look so shocked. Everyone knew about it. Though perhaps some sooner than others." Now there was an edge to her words.

The accusation was clear, and Ash bowed his head. "I should have told you sooner."

"You should have told me first."

Ash could not deny it. He nodded, quiet in the face of her equally quiet anger. Amarillya's fingers clenched tight, and he watched the emotions dart over her face before she brought them under control. Fury. Hurt. Regret.

"And just what do you propose to do about it?" she asked him then.

"Beg your forgiveness. If not for now, then in time. Whenever you're ready to give it."

"And?"

"Have Lelande speak with your father, alone. Speak with him myself, if he demands it. Amarillya, I cannot marry you."

"Obviously."

He struggled to explain, to assure her that the shame was his, that he had not dishonored her completely. "Ren and I—we haven't . . . I've never . . ."

Amarillya did not flush or avert her gaze at what he alluded. Instead she gave an impatient snort, surprising him. "Clearly, or you would not be in this mess to begin with." Her tone was sarcastic. "Do you really think I care about any of that? I almost wish you *had* lain with Ren. At least then, nobody else would have needed to put up with your utter stupidity. Other than Ren himself, of course."

Hardly daring to hope, Ash wisely kept his mouth shut as Amarillya sighed, then walked toward him.

"You love him, I suppose?"

He nodded.

"Say it then."

"I love him. I love Ren."

Another soft gust of wind filled the room at his words. The curtains billowed, and Ash breathed in the scent of wood and leaf, sap and soil.

Amarillya stopped in front of him, close enough for them to touch. Leaning forward, she kissed a now dumbfounded Ash on the cheek. "Idiot," she said, almost affectionately, then made her way to the door and pointedly opened it. "I will speak to Father myself. Perhaps he will be angry, but in time he will see it was for the best. He must."

Ash marveled at her strength. Despite all he had done, and all he had not, Amarillya was making it easier for him.

"Amarillya . . . thank you. For everything." There was a tight lump in Ash's throat and a prickling behind his eyelids. "And I really am sorry."

"Don't be. I very much doubt it would have worked out between us anyway. Don't you agree?" She was carefully looking away as she waited for him to take his leave.

"Amarillya?" A thought occurred to him when he was half-way out of the room, and he quickly turned back to her while he still had the chance to be alone in her presence. "Koresh. You should call on him sometime, or have him call on you. I think he would like that."

"Koresh?" Amarillya looked at him, brows drawn for a moment, before Ash saw a flash of understanding pass over her face. "Perhaps I will. Sometime." She nodded politely. "Farewell, Ash."

She did not wait for his reply, and Ash made sure to walk quickly away so that he might say with all honesty he had not heard any sound, either of grief or anger, coming from the room once he had departed.

He rode straight home, determinedly not lingering or gazing out at the road leading north.

It did not mean all of his demons had been laid to rest. In the wake of what had occurred between him and Amarillya, Ash could not settle to anything. His continued lessons with Mara did not distract him enough, and nor did any of the books on the subject in the library that Lelande pointedly directed him toward. In truth, Ash no longer particularly cared whether his Gift would return to him or not. Many among the nobility were unGifted — what did it matter if Ash was numbered among them? Besides, since being Gifted was largely thought of as an added sign of status, he could see no reason why he of all people was deserving of such abilities in the first place. Still, for his older brother's sake, he continued to try.

This was difficult when his mind was so unruly, his thoughts constantly scattering like windblown leaves in his head. Coming to a full understanding of what it was Ash felt for Ren and actually saying it out loud were two very different things, and he knew that if it had been difficult to say to Amarillya, it would be far more difficult to admit to Ren himself.

Still, spending so much in the company of books had at least given Ash an idea.

And so he scrawled his thoughts, inelegant and disordered as they were, on tiny scraps of parchment as they came to him. In doing so he found that, after all, what he had to say in one moment could be fitted neatly within the fold of a robe, or beneath a candle by the window in the next.

He placed these thoughts in Ren's chamber, some hidden away, others recklessly visible.

I'm sorry found its way into the pocket of an old cloak hanging in the wardrobe. *I miss you* was tucked safely inside a drawer, bare but for a wax tablet and stylus. *Come home soon* was half-buried beneath a mound of small river stones placed in a bowl on a shelf. He whispered these things to the empty room and hoped they would be enough to see Ren safely back.

Only one message was not written down in Ash's untidy hand, for he knew this at least must be spoken aloud, no matter how much embarrassment it caused him.

At night, Ash continued to sleep in Ren's bedchamber, uncaring as to what anyone else thought of this strange behavior if they knew of it, and wondering just what Ren might have to say about it if he did.

Ash was dreaming.

He knew he must be still sleeping because Ren was there — not doing or saying anything, just sitting beside him, unmoving and staring at Ash, his face too shadowed to make out his expression. It was not like in Ash's previous dreams about Ren, where he had been doing plenty more than just sitting there, and with far less in the way of clothing on — but because Ash had never truly seen Ren in any state other than utterly composed, excepting of course for the few times Ash had incited him to fear or rage, he did not doubt that what he saw now could be anything but a dream.

Ren's clothes had streaks of dirt on them, faint but obvious, and he had never dared appear before Ash in anything that was not immaculately clean. But there they were — dark smudges here and there, what looked like a grass stain or two marring the fabric, flecks of mud still clinging to his boots. His hair was damp and windswept, small strands wet enough to stick to his forehead. In the light of the flickering candle that had not yet sputtered out, Ash could see that even Ren's face was not quite free from the vestiges of his journey, and was speckled with dirt.

He almost smiled to witness this other side of Ren — a side of him that, in reality, he would never have allowed Ash to see.

"Ren." Ash's voice crept sleepily from his mouth as Ren

shifted imperceptibly on his chair next to the bed.

Ren's eyes were dark and unreadable, and Ash hesitated before reminding himself that this was not actually happening, that Ren was not really here. Knowing this, he allowed himself to speak selfishly. Honestly.

"Don't leave me again," he pleaded, and tentatively reached out a hand. "Please?"

For one awful moment, his hand met only air. Then it was firmly grasped in a paler one—a hand that was cool and calloused, and had dirt under the fingernails.

Even in Ash's most tangible and lurid of dreams, Ren had never been more desirable.

This was Ash's final thought as his eyes closed again. If Ren made any reply to his request, Ash did not remember hearing it.

But in the morning, the chair was still there, and the candle had been lined up next to the waxy stumps of the rest that Ash had burned, one for each night he had passed in Ren's bedchamber.

I'll still be here.

The note, penned in Ren's own careful hand, was waiting for him where he had been sitting, neatly folded and placed on top of all the rest of the notes Ren had found.

Ash paced outside the closed door. From within, Lelande was speaking in low, measured tones. He could not make out what his brother was saying, or the even quieter replies that Ren gave in return, and did not attempt to eavesdrop. While in the past he might have been more curious, Ash now found he would rather not know.

It was late morning, and after waking to find that his only vaguely-remembered dream had not been a dream after all, Ash had thought his heart might leap from his chest if it started to beat any harder. He couldn't decide whether to be mortified or elated upon finding that Ren had not only discovered all the notes Ash had written him over the past few days, but responded with one of his own.

Ash hadn't thought it was possible for a body to hold so much nervousness all at once. His fingers were tingling with it, and he wasn't sure if he had gone very red or very white. His breath came in little half-gasps as though he had been running, although his feet felt rooted to the floor whenever he managed to force himself to stop pacing.

He was still standing in the exact same spot when the door opened.

Lelande looked only mildly surprised to see Ash waiting there. His older brother's face showed tiredness, but little else that Ash could make out, as he took in Ash's state of dread with a practiced glance. "I see you are aware Ren has returned," he said dryly.

Ash nodded, suddenly unable to speak, and Lelande sighed, pinching the bridge of his nose between thumb and forefinger. "Well. He's all yours." There was a hint of irony beneath the weary tone.

Ash's eyes widened. "What did you—"

But Lelande was already walking past him down the hallway and did not look back at Ash's query.

He had left the door open. From beyond it, Ash could hear footsteps, although the person within was still out of sight. Ash swallowed, pushing the door open further.

Ren was standing by the window, his body little more than a silhouette against the brightness of the sun streaming through the glass. His face was smooth and unreadable, his gaze just as inscrutable as it had been when he had been watching Ash several hours ago.

"My lord—no. Ash." Ren sounded deeply uncertain, every bit as nervous as Ash was sure he himself looked, but at the sound of his name on Ren's lips, Ash felt a giddy burst of relief.

"It's so good to see you, Ren." He made no attempt to disguise the depth of feeling with which he spoke the words.

Ren shifted, an unfamiliar, jerky motion, and since Ash could not read his expression, he glanced further down instead — saw the way Ren's shoulders were held taut, his back straight and stiff, his feet shifting as though even now he wanted to begin pacing just as Ash had been only moments ago.

"Do you . . . are we..?"

"Yes," Ash replied stupidly, and crossed the room so that he stood close enough to look at Ren properly.

Blue-gray eyes looked back at him, neither cool nor closed off, but instead bright with some emotion Ren apparently could not put into words. Not yet, anyway. But there would be time enough to learn — time enough for both of them.

"You're back."

"This is my home." Ren's voice was husky.

Ash found he could not stop smiling. "Welcome home."

CHAPTER SIX

It was raining — a light, warm drizzle that smelled of freshly dampened earth — the night Ash came once again to Ren's bedchamber, this time with Ren inside of it. He shivered, fear and anticipation mingling together.

Ren saw this as Ash closed the door behind him. "Ash. We don't have to do this now, tonight — there's no need to rush anything. It can wait. *We* can wait."

Ash shook his head. "The longer I wait, the more afraid I'll be," he admitted. "I want this — I do. It's just — I don't think I'll ever stop being . . . until you and I . . ." He swallowed, trying to push past his fear.

After Ren's return to the manor, it had taken days, weeks more to lead up to this point, to where they stood now, alone and facing each other. The thought of physical intimacy was separated from the act by what felt like little more than a breath. Despite the fact that Ash was now capable of expressing much of what he felt, and that Ren had made it plain those feelings were reciprocated, both needed time to speak and to listen, and to get used to being in one another's presence again, this time while knowing full well what it was that lay between them.

This had not always been easy, especially when old habits threatened to get in the way. Far less awkward, surely, for Ash to seek solitude among the forested mountain paths than give words to his feelings, or for Ren to channel his own feelings into his training, allowing Ash to see only the side of himself that was coolly detached and self-possessed. Both were still adjusting to the feeling of being naked in front of one another, even when fully clothed.

But Ash loved Ren even more, if such a thing was possible, when he spoke not only of his love but also of his fears.

"I thought you would not wish to touch me if you knew," Ren admitted once, softly, as though still ashamed even now. "I didn't want to be touched by you either, knowing how I felt and thinking you would never feel the same. That it was selfish of me to want, when I had already been given a place, a home, that I had done nothing to earn. And I thought that if anyone ever found out, if Lelande ever knew what I wanted to do, how I desired . . ." Ren swallowed, his eyes darting about as if afraid to alight on Ash's face. "His own brother, his flesh and blood. He would do anything to protect you, to protect his family. For me to jeopardize that . . . I was so afraid of being sent away from the only place I had ever known that made me happy. I was afraid of being sent away from *you*."

Ren had only calmed when Ash pulled him close, stroking his hair and marveling at its softness despite how closely cut it was, murmuring his reply into Ren's ear, flushing as he did so. "Nobody will send you away. This is your home, too, don't you know that? Don't you think everybody knows that?" And then, when he felt Ren's heartbeat finally begin to slow: "I loved you for years, wanted you and dreamed about you for years in ways I couldn't even . . ." He stumbled over the words, his entire body burning now, but knowing they were important, no matter how much embarrassment they caused him. "I wanted to ask you so many things, wanted to know everything there was to know about you. I still do. Will you tell me? Not just about now, but about before? About your childhood and growing up in the capital?"

Ren stilled for a moment, then seemed to make an effort to relax, his body growing softer as he leaned into Ash. " . . . Yes. Not right now, but someday, I will. I promise you that. Will you wait?"

"Of course I will." He could feel Ren's heart pounding, but Ash only continued to hold him. Whatever lay in his past, Ash would not let it come between them, and Ren's vulnerabilities only made Ash want him all the more.

This night, Ren was outwardly calm as they stood in alone his bedchamber, the manor silent about them and the darkness outside cloaking them together in privacy. His voice was steady, but his eyes spoke a different message.

"You know there's nothing I would do if you didn't want it as well. If there was anything you didn't like, something that made you feel . . . threatened, or afraid, no matter what it was . . ."

Ren's eyes searched Ash's face as if trying to gauge his resolve, gain some measure of how much of the tension that gripped him was true apprehension.

Ash made himself meet that look steadily. Long before Osias, he had imagined this, acknowledged his desire and his aching, empty body, and had gone on desiring even when he thought nothing could come of it. He did not want his own fear over what had taken place to come between them now, just when he had finally discovered that Ren was never as unaffected as he appeared. Not when it was now only hunger that lay thick and heavy between them.

"It's all right. I'm ready. Please, Ren." It was true — he had never felt more ready for anything in his life. Though the dark still made him skittish, he knew he was safe with Ren.

He felt another tremor run through him when Ren moved closer and reached out to begin undressing him. He did not seem to mind when Ash fumbled as he tried to reciprocate. As Ren paused to touch the different parts of Ash's body that were gradually bared to the night — sometimes only brushing with the tips of his fingers, sometimes kissing softly, once even biting, carefully controlled, near the hollow of Ash's throat, making him jump—Ash slowly forgot his fear.

As each article of clothing was abandoned, more and more of their skin freed to press and graze against one another, Ren sighed Ash's name as though making up for all the times he had not spoken it.

Ash's own skin felt alien to him, as though it belonged to someone else, and when Ren's kisses turned more fervent, he could not help himself, freezing in half-remembered fright. "Ren?"

Ren drew away at once. "Yes?"

"Will it . . . will it hurt?" He wanted to die of embarrassment as the question slipped out, tremulous and baring every inch of his painful inexperience, despite the knowledge that Ren could hardly be much more experienced himself.

But Ren did not laugh or brush off Ash's fear. He only gathered Ash in his arms and drew him close. "Not tonight. I swear it."

Ash's skin burned when Ren went back to kissing him, heating up wherever he was touched, and at some point he must have remembered to touch back, because Ren groaned and his breath grew harder.

The feel of the bed against Ash's legs came as a surprise—he hadn't realized Ren had been guiding them backward until he found himself there. Even as they half-lay, half-fell onto the mattress, Ash remained entranced, his hands roaming Ren's body and mapping out the firm chest, the broad shoulders, enjoying the weight of him.

If Ash had been worried once about how Ren might see him, overly tall and awkward, scrawny and inelegant and all that a lord should not have been, he was not so now. Ren made no secret of his desire, the way his hardness pressed against Ash's legs. It astonished and delighted Ash, that someone usually so reserved and undecipherable could look the way Ren looked at him now.

"*Ash.*" His name was spoken with reverence and some amazement, as though Ren had never dared imagine he might call him by it—not like this, flesh pressed to naked flesh, Ash gasping and writhing beneath him.

Just like they had in his dreams, one calloused hand moved to take Ash's hands over his head and hold them there—not hard enough to hurt or to keep Ash from moving if he really wanted to, but with enough pressure that Ash could feel the strength and the hunger in his grasp. It excited Ash, made him want more, and he jerked and cried out when their bodies met and ground together.

But his earlier visions were only pale imitations of what was happening now—his imagination was nothing compared to the kind of hunger Ren aroused in Ash in return. His back arched from the bed, Ren's touch making him blaze with it. It didn't have a name—only a sound, or a hundred different sounds, that crowded at Ash's throat, to be released only when Ren stroked *here* and bit *oh gods there*, making Ash thrust back impatiently.

He was hard and damp, his breathing erratic, and he no longer cared what he looked or sounded like so long as Ren just kept moving like that, a rhythm that began steadily and then spiraled into something fast and fierce, powerful and desperate. Ash struggled automatically to match it until the friction became almost unbearable, a surge of energy that caused him to toss his head and dig his nails into Ren's back, clinging as the dizziness swept over him.

Helpless, he moaned, twisting in pleasure and begging for more, more. Ren gave it to him, whispering into Ash's ear, a soft counterpoint to his tightly controlled grip.

"Beautiful, you're beautiful, you don't know how I want you—"

It was like bursting out, like falling upward, Ren's hands on him and holding him as he crashed into wakefulness. It was like a gust of wind strong enough to shake him and leave him breathless and shuddering, a tree trembling in the midst of a storm.

"Ash . . . Ash . . ." Ren was calling his name again, softly now but still a little amazed, still awed by the sound of it.

Ash opened his eyes to stare up at him, wondering at the fact that in all that tempest of feeling, the world about them was somehow the same as he had left it. The chamber was still dim, the bed still a solid presence cradling his back, the rain still drumming quietly at the window. Nothing had changed.

Only everything had, because Ash could feel the weight of Ren's body over his own, hands rubbing carefully at his wrists, making sure Ash was not bruised. He saw himself reflected in Ren's eyes, naked and flushed and exposed, and felt no shame in it—only a kind of peace that seemed to extend down to the core of him.

"Will you stay with me tonight?" The words emerged from Ren's mouth a little shyly, making Ash fall in love with him all over again, though Ren's hands were still idly stroking.

"I . . . might have been sleeping in your chamber all the time you were away," Ash admitted.

"I know." Ren smiled, his mouth gently curving, and Ash was so entranced by it that he almost forgot to feel embarrassed.

"How?"

Ren considered. "The smell, I suppose."

Ash spluttered, red-faced, protesting.

"Not a bad smell. Just you." Ren inhaled now, unexpectedly, tickling Ash's still sensitized skin. "Like good, clean earth. Like root and stem and the rain on the wind."

"Oh," Ash mumbled. "Well then."

"Yes." Ren fumbled with the blankets until they were both more or less covered, their bodies still pressed closely against one another. If he had grown red from his own words, Ash could not see in the dimness. "You're certain you don't mind?"

"No." It felt delicious, being this close to Ren like they had once before, only this time warm and cozy and in a bed instead of wet and shivering in a cave. "Why would I?"

"I thought you hated the idea of losing your privacy. Or at least, that's what I swear I remember you saying when we first met. *So I'm to be followed around for the rest of my life?* Or something to that effect."

Ren looked as though he was holding back a smile, and Ash narrowed his eyes suspiciously. " . . . Are you teasing me?"

"Yes." The smile was hidden no longer, and Ash knew he would never tire of it, no matter how much Ren wanted to tease him.

"Well in that case." Ash yawned, struggling against a tide of pleasant exhaustion and wriggled closer. "We'll have to work on your delivery another time. Who knows, maybe one day you'll even work your way up to telling an entire joke."

He might have imagined the quiet laughter near his ear. "Yes, my lord."

"Ash," he admonished, but his eyes were already closing.

"Yes, Ash."

He would never tire of that either — not from Ren.

Ash smiled and glanced over at the only candle still left burning, lazily waving his hand at it but not truly expecting much, or even really caring. Then he closed his eyes, aware that even if the world itself had not changed, he at least had. The truth of it sank down to his very bones.

Resting on the table near the window, the candle's flame wavered in an unseen puff of wind and flickered silently out.

EPILOGUE

One year later . . .

"And where are you going so late in the afternoon?" Lelande stopped Ash at the door, one eyebrow raised.

"Oh, nowhere really. Just out." Ash tried for a nonchalant tone and failed, shuffling his feet awkwardly. "Ren's coming too," he added.

"Ah." The corners of Lelande's mouth twitched. "Well, don't be too late in returning, either of you. We have guests arriving, remember?"

"I remember." He hadn't, but wasn't about to say so to Lelande—especially since he could see Koresh out of the corner of his eye, hovering on the staircase and looking uncharacteristically nervous. "Don't worry, Koresh. Amarillya isn't likely to turn you down, even if I spoil dinner by being late."

"Who said I was going to ask Amarillya anything?" Koresh snapped, but his face was turning a telltale red. "And you'd better *not* be late," he added quickly as Ren passed him coming down the stairs.

"We will not, my lord."

"Well." Koresh looked somewhat mollified at Ren's assured tone. "See to it, then."

"Ash, wait!" Aria dashed out from where she had been taking a lesson in another room with Mara, who followed somewhat more sedately behind. Aria's Gift had made itself known some weeks earlier, and she had been beside herself with the knowledge that she too had the same ability as her

106

brothers to *talk to the wind,* as she put it. "What if it rains? Mara said she can smell it on the air." She sniffed, trying to see if she too could smell it.

"Maybe it's easier to tell if you're standing outside," Ren offered, and Aria half-ran to the door, opening it and inhaling deeply.

"I still can't smell anything."

"Perhaps the rain changed its mind," Mara said, catching up with her, one wrinkled hand absentmindedly patting her shoulder. "But take care anyway, you two. It would not do to be caught in a sudden storm . . . now would it?"

Ash reddened, but Ren showed no reaction to these last words. "We will." He turned to Lelande. "I'll see us back in plenty of time, my lord."

"I know you will." Lelande did not appear concerned, although Mara looked suspiciously amused at Ash's sudden discomfort.

"Let's go." Not wanting to give anyone a chance to say anything more, he tugged Ren out the door, eager to be away.

Ren smiled and allowed himself to be pulled along. "Why the rush? The river will still be there in the morning."

"Yes, but I want to walk by it *now.* Besides, I think Mara's actually right—it will start to rain soon, and you know how it can get. It might not let up for a few days."

"And when has that ever stopped you?"

"It hasn't." Ash colored again, remembering the first time they had been trapped out of doors in the pouring rain. "But that doesn't mean I actually enjoy getting soaked."

"You might have fooled me." Ren glanced back at the door, seeing it was still open, then closed a hand around Ash's anyway, raising it to his lips. "Come, then. I wouldn't blame Koresh for what he might do to you if we were late coming back. Nor Amarillya, come to that."

"I suppose you may have a point."

Ren bowed ironically. "My lord."

"None of that." Ash grabbed Ren's hand again as they set off toward the river, the breeze already teasing wisps of hair free from its binding and the dinner already far from his mind. For now, his only concern was this — the mountains rising up, tall and green like a protective circle on either side of him, the feel of Ren's fingers tangled comfortably about his own.

The wind whispered over his skin.

He was truly home.

YOU MAY ALSO ENJOY THE FOLLOWING FROM EXTASY BOOKS INC:

Kaidyn's Courage
Diana Waters

Excerpt

Kaidyn was running.

Boots thumping on the uneven cobblestones, he darted around townspeople. He ran past rows of street merchants loudly hawking their wares, a band of children playing games with small colored stones, a pair of squabbling old women.

A hunk of meat was roasting on a spit, its owner trying — and failing — to keep the flies away. A small gang of sharp-eyed boys watched passersby, perhaps on the lookout for a rich pocket to pick, while a group of heavily bearded men threw cards at a rickety table. Nearby, a baby wailed in the arms of a woman who might have been its mother or its sister, attempting in vain to quiet it.

Not a drop of rain had fallen in weeks, and the earth was dry as a bone. Swirling dust and dirt and gods knew what else made Kaidyn want to shield his mouth. All the surrounding sights, smells, and sounds enveloped him, swallowing him up until he was just one of many, vanishing in the swarm of bodies.

Somewhere in front and a little to the right of him, Luck let out an exuberant whoop as though he was running a race instead of running from his superiors. "Lost 'em, Kai!" he shouted above the din. He slowed around the next corner and Kaidyn caught up to walk alongside him, eventually stopping to lean up against the shade of a twisted door frame. Luck thumped down beside him, grinning. "Told you it would work."

Kaidyn felt the corners of his mouth tilt upwards in response despite himself. "You did," he agreed. "Care to tell me how you escaped your own quarters?"

"Maybe I came up with such a good distraction they never even saw me leave."

Kaidyn raised an eyebrow.

"Or maybe I seduced one of the guards," Luck continued, batting his eyelashes in an unconvincing display of flirtatiousness. "Hinted at my many charms."

"Really."

"Oh, all right. Someone did show off their charms, but it wasn't me. I called in a favor from a friend. A very well-endowed friend, if you must know."

"Ah. That makes more sense." Luck's particular brand of roguish appeal had always made him popular with women, though this one might have been anything from a passing acquaintance to a lover. He often visited the brothels and was familiar with many of the workers there, men and women both.

"I'll have you know I happen to be very seductive when I put my mind to it."

"I'm sure."

Luck grinned again, pushing unruly curls from his eyes.

Though Kaidyn didn't say it, he had missed his childhood friend. Now that they were separated by different training schools, it had been several weeks since their last meeting.

As far as Kaidyn was concerned, Luck had been one of the sole joys to result from moving permanently to the capital as a child. The looming threat of war with Iskandir had finally become serious enough for the family to abandon their less grand yet far more private summer palace in the north. By comparison, the capital had seemed overly large and unfriendly. Even his sister, whom Kaidyn had idolized, appeared to grow cold and remote almost overnight.

The other children living in and around the palace were minor relatives and little lords or ladies in their own right. They took cues from their elders and kept their distance from him. Everyone was aware that although Kaidyn was a prince, he was unable to inherit, even had he been the eldest child. Anyone in good standing knew the Half-Blood would never have any significant role in matters of state or the court. His father's ancestry saw to that.

But Luck had been as different from them as day from night. Tall and lanky, he was a slightly wild boy even then with his head of shorn, tight brown curls and laughing eyes almost exactly the same shade as Kaidyn's own. If not for his distinctly rough manner of speech, they might even have passed as brothers. Certainly Kaidyn resembled Luck far more than he did Lyrah, who was as small as her mother, but had inherited her late father's slenderness and sea-green eyes. Kaidyn had been in awe of his new friend, so different from any other he had known and with an unquestionable talent for getting into trouble—and usually for skipping neatly out of it again.

They had been utterly inseparable in their youth. As children they had been thick as thieves and cared nothing for their difference in status. When they were together, Kaidyn, the son of the queen, was equal to Luck, the son of an undercook who worked somewhere in the palace's vast kitchens.

As the years passed, however, they experienced a growing awareness of who and what they were in the eyes of the court. They made a pact not to care about status and shared a friendly rivalry, fighting over which of them could run quicker, ride faster or fight harder.

As young men on the verge of adulthood, they had for a brief time become lovers in the way many others did who trained or fought away from home. Now, they were closer to brothers again, protective and goading in equal measures, and determined to fight the world together.

Luck was still catching his breath as Kaidyn cast a glance from their makeshift hiding place. He could neither see nor hear any sign of pursuit, though no doubt at least one or two of his instructors were among the crowd somewhere, attempting to track him down like some runaway child. Well, they would be searching a long time. Kaidyn had no intention of returning until much later, long after darkness had fallen and he would not be bothered by anyone.

With some luck, he might even be able to sleep a few hours, uninterrupted by others and his ugly thoughts. Even in the light of day they had a habit of stealing into his head, making his gut turn sour, his hands curl into fists —

"C'mon, I need a drink." Luck pushed himself back from the door frame. "On you this time. I'm your dashing savior, after all, helping you break out of there like the delicate young flower you are."

Kaidyn grunted but nodded, even as an unwelcome sense of responsibility nagged at him. He was, despite everything, a son of the royal family as well as a soldier, and his actions reflected on them. He shouldn't be worrying his mother, shaming his sister, giving the Council yet another reason to despise him by shirking his duties.

"You're doing it again." Luck jostled him playfully, scattering his thoughts.

"Doing what?"

"Overthinking it."

Kaidyn made a conscious effort to relax his shoulders and allowed Luck to sweep them back out into the milling throng. They walked at a slower pace, the crowd swarming around Kaidyn as he trailed behind Luck, who led the way to one of their frequent drinking spots. It was not the first time they had passed an evening in such a way — and it would almost certainly not be the last.

But Kaidyn could not fault Luck for trying to distract him and knew that however isolated he might feel, he was not alone in his sense of entrapment. It was like a noose, one that gradually tightened day by day as empty, faceless spectators hissed and jeered. They spat on him, just as they spat on Luck for being somehow lesser than they were in the world. Nobody ever bothered to say less what exactly, but Kaidyn already knew without having to be told.

Less noble. Less worthy. Less honorable. A half-breed, with the blood of an enemy nation flowing through his veins. It would have been one thing simply to be unGifted, as many nobles were no matter how high their rank. It was quite another to be a physical reminder to all who looked upon him of his race.

But for all that, he was no noble's pet to whimper and cower, or worse, beg in an effort to please or placate his so-called betters. He would turn on his masters and sink his teeth into their flesh before such a day ever came.

Suddenly aware his fingernails had been digging into his palm again, Kaidyn let out a breath in an explosive sigh. At least the tavern would be loud enough that he wouldn't be able to hear himself think. What was one more drink to try and make him forget for a time?

And so he pushed the uninvited thoughts away and followed Luck further into the crowd.

ABOUT THE AUTHOR

Diana is a New Zealand M/M romance author currently residing in New York. However, she has also lived and worked
for several years in Japan and several months in Thailand. She
has no idea where in the world she'll be this time next year
and is pretty okay with that. Other than reading and writing,
her main passions include international travel, amateur pho-
tography and competitive swimming.

www.ingramcontent.com/pod-product-compliance
Lightning Source LLC
Chambersburg PA
CBHW060642130626
46555CB00002B/919